DAUGHTER OF THE RIVERS

DAUGHTER OF THE RIVERS

ILKO MINEV

TRANSLATED BY DIANE GROSKLAUS WHITTY

Daugther of the Rivers
Published by Eriginal Books LLC
Miami, Florida
www.eriginalbooks.com
www.eriginalbooks.net

Original Title: A Filha Dos Rios
First edition, 2015
Second edition, 2016

Painting on the cover: Téo Braga

Author's Website: www.ilkominev.com

ISBN: 978-1-61370-076-1

CONTENTS

CHAPTER 1
FROM PURUS TO ABUNÃ

The young man sitting in the bow of the small canoe had been rowing at the same pace for hours. He was traveling down a long, narrow channel that linked the Purus River to Lake Igapó-Mirim, which, word had it, abounded in all types of fish. He'd have to catch something as soon as he reached the lake. He hadn't eaten in almost twelve hours. At long last, the lush vegetation opened up as sunlight penetrated the swamp forest. He was just about there. The water was so dark it was nearly black, a sure sign it was clean and safe to drink. Without missing a beat of his paddle, he tossed a small hook, tied to a feather, into the water a few yards behind the canoe. It didn't take long. As he was entering the lake, the man felt a tug on his nylon line. He'd snagged a small piranha. It wouldn't make a whole meal for a fellow his size, so he threw the bait back in and waited for another hit. Soon he'd nabbed another small piranha. It was only on the third try that a bigger fish took the bait—a peacock bass, another predator typical to the region.

Now the young man had food enough and just needed to find some dry land in the midst of the swamps that form every year during the season of high waters. This wasn't as easy as it might sound. He rowed and rowed but couldn't find a single place where he could get out of his canoe, make a fire, and roast his fish. Then, in the middle of nowhere, he spied a small wooden house floating atop a platform of immense possumwood logs. As he drew closer, he saw it was inhabited. There was a dog and even a small garden.

"This fellow's on the ball," he thought, as he slid his canoe alongside the house The mutt kept barking away and some folks soon came out of the house—five kids of assorted ages and a wisp of a woman, probably no more than thirty but looking much older, her features typical of a denizen of the riverside.

"I'm new around here, ma'am," he said. "My name's Adriano. I'm looking for a spot of dry land where I can roast a fish and spend the night."

"You're going to look hard and not find any. This time of year, we got no riverbanks round here. Dry land—only find it along the Purus," the woman replied. "You can climb aboard and stretch your legs."

From the height of the floating deck, Adriano could see two canoes at rest in the middle of the harbor, a ways off. Their occupants were shooting arrows straight up into the air, one right after the other, non-stop.

"What're they doing?" Adriano asked. "They after turtles?"

Adriano had seen fellows going after tortoises and river turtles a few times. They'd figure in the arc of the arrow and shoot straight up. When the arrow landed, it

8

would hit the shell full force. If you aimed straight on, it never worked, even if you hit the creature. The arrow would simply glance off its smooth hard shell.

"No. They're right above a school of flagtail. Ain't even aiming, just shooting the arrows up. When they come down, almost always get something. Lots of fish there," said the lady of the house. "My name's Eulália."

"Maybe I can help. I've got a casting net in the canoe and I can throw good."

"Better to wait. It's about time for Maria and Antônio to be heading back. Especially since they must've heard the dog barking."

The canoes did return shortly. Manned by a middle-aged *caboclo*,[1] one was plumb full of fish. A dark-skinned girl paddled the other one; she was toasted by the sun, her face lit by two startlingly green eyes.

"Ma, Antônio got too many fish. They're going to rot in this heat."

The girl ignored the stranger and went straight into the house. Without a word, Antônio made dock, tied up his canoe, and before getting out, asked in a sharp voice, "Who are you?"

"My name's Adriano. I'm the son of Renildo Antunes and Dona[2] Selma, from the town of Lábrea."

"What you doing in our lake?"

---

[1] T.N.: In the context of this book, a native of the Amazon region. *Caboclo*: male, singular. *Cabocla*: female, singular. *Caboclos*: male or mixed gender, plural. *Caboclas*: female, plural.

[2] T.N.: Honorific used before a woman's first name.

"I'm canoeing down the Purus, headed to Manaus. I need a place to spend the night," Adriano replied.

"Can't be here. This lake's got an owner," Antônio cut in.

"I just wanted to roast a fish and catch some sleep. I'll be gone tomorrow."

"Where you leave the lake at the other end, there's an abandoned houseboat. You can roast your fish and spend the night there." Antônio pointed to the other side, a long way off.

There was nothing more to say so Adriano got back into his canoe. He waved goodbye and headed slowly in the direction Antônio had pointed.

The older man looked relieved. He hadn't liked the appearance of the intruder, especially since he'd seen a shotgun in the bottom of the stranger's canoe and knew he wasn't unarmed.

ΦΦΦ

It took Adriano nearly an hour to locate what was left of the abandoned houseboat. It would do for the night but offered no protection against bad weather. It had no walls, no roof—just a wood raft atop two massive possumwood logs. It was enough for lighting a fire and roasting the fish. The traveler fell asleep as the first stars came out.

Men of the forest never sleep deeply, and in the middle of the night, Adriano heard the muffled sound of paddles cutting through water, distant at first but drawing ever closer. The moon was full and he could see clearly all around him. He reached quietly for his loaded gun, slid into the canoe, and pushed it behind the houseboat. Adriano soon realized he could hear more than one canoe and the rowers weren't trying to sneak up—much to the contrary, they were making more noise than necessary. Two canoes came out of the shadows and slipped up to the houseboat.

"The stranger's left already!" Adriano heard the voice of Dona Eulália.

"No, Ma. I can see him hiding in the woods, scared out of his wits," the girl replied snidely.

"I'm here, and I'm not afraid," Adriano piped up. "I just didn't know who was coming."

"I need to talk to you, stranger. And I have to make it quick." Eulália had no time to waste. She stayed in her canoe and cut straight to the heart of the matter.

"Maria's my daughter from before I got together with Antônio. She's growing up now and can't stay around here anymore. I seen the way Antônio looks at the girl, spying on her when she bathes or changes. I know he's going to go after her any day now. Maria's already got her period, so she's a woman now," Eulália explained. "She's got to get away from here before something nasty happens."

Adriano stared at the young girl. She didn't budge or say a word. Even in the moonlight it was easy to see she was an adolescent. Dressed in a pair of Adidas shorts, she looked more like a boy than a woman. Her budding breasts contrasted with her worn T-shirt and were the only feminine thing about her.

"Get her out of here before it's too late. Antônio downed some *cachaça*[3] and he's going to be asleep for a while, time enough for me to get back. I'm going to get a good beating, even if I say I don't know a thing and that Maria just up and snuck off in one of the canoes. I'm going to hide all our paddles too. It'll take him ages to find them and by then you'll both be far away."

"I got myself in a fine kettle of fish," Adriano thought. "She's not giving me any choice. She didn't even ask whether I want the kid!"

Doubt-filled as he was, Adriano surprised even himself by saying, "Where's her things? We'll leave right away. My canoe gets heavy and slow with two in it. What's her full name?"

"She's just got one change of clothes." The mother put a small bundle and a bow and arrows in the bottom of his canoe. "Maria's the dolphin's daughter. I was just a little thing, younger than her now, when I met him. He was disguised as a fisherman. His name was Reinaldo, and she gets her green eyes from him. He never came back and don't know about the child. No clue where he's at, or even if he's alive. Maria hasn't got papers, never did register her."

---

[3] T.N.: A type of hard liquor made from sugar cane, similar to rum.

Adriano understood perfectly well what Dona Eulália was talking about. The Amazon riverbanks were home to many sons and daughters of the enchanted dolphin. So went the legend that explained how children were born without a father, often the result of a brief love affair between a naïve young girl of the river and some silver-tongued stranger passing through.

Mother and daughter hugged each other and Maria climbed into Adriano's canoe.

"I'll come back one day and bring your daughter, Dona Eulália. But one more thing. How old is she?"

"She turns 16 soon," the mother replied, and for a second Adriano thought he saw tears in her eyes. Despite the full moon, there wasn't enough light for him to be sure.

Maria started paddling their canoe towards the channel that led out of the lake, while Eulália went off in the opposite direction, without looking back.

"The girl only looks frail, but she's strong and handles a paddle well," noted Adriano. That's when he heard a sob and realized Maria could barely choke back her tears. He put his hand on her shoulder, hoping to comfort her.

"Don't touch me!" the girl shouted. Sharing the small space of the canoe with this wild creature was obviously not going to be easy.

"I'm not going to touch you. We'll paddle to the town of Manacapuru, on the Solimões River, and then we'll decide what to do. The first thing is to get you registered. The way things are now, you don't even exist. In Manacapuru, or maybe Manaus, we can try to find a place for you."

She said nothing, and they continued to paddle along in silence towards the great river. Until this point in time, Maria's small world had been limited to the lake where she was born. She'd never been so far away.

ΦΦΦ

The forest awoke with the sun's first rays. Hurried egrets and noisy parrots popped out all over. The young girl watched in astonishment as the thick forest dropped away and the canoe slid down a huge rush of yellow water, the great Purus River. On the one hand, it was easier to row, because the river's strong current swept the canoe along. On the other, the waves were bigger than any Maria had ever seen. They spent the day paddling, not even stopping to eat. It was only in the late afternoon that Adriano pulled ashore in a harbor—it was actually the mouth of a small lake—and announced: "We'll spend the night here. I'm going fishing in the lake while you make a fire and hang the hammock. I'll be back with fish and clean water."

Adriano was skilled with a casting net and had soon caught more than enough fish for their next meal. When he got back, he was happy to see a fire burning and the hammock strung up.

He was surprised when Maria asked for the canoe. She rowed into the small lake and Adriano watched from afar as she jumped into the water. He laughed to himself, because he'd done the same thing. It had been a hot, physically strenuous day. Unlike the muddy Purus River, the dark, clean waters of the lakes around it were incomparably soothing, and diving into them was the best way to relax and wash off the sweat. A dolphin swam so close it almost brushed against Maria, but she showed no alarm. She was used to them.

They ate dinner in silence. They hadn't exchanged more than half a dozen words all day, each one watching the other.

Adriano broke the silence. "We've got only one hammock. We'll have to sleep in it. Don't worry, I won't touch you."

"I found a blue tarp in the canoe," she countered, referring to the small piece of oilcloth Adriano used to protect himself from the rain. "I'll sleep in it."

"Well, seeing as you don't trust me, I'll sleep in the tarp and you can have the hammock," he decided quickly. "I'm going to dowse the fire. Hard to sleep with so many mosquitoes."

"I don't know what we're going to do when it rains," a tired Adriano thought as he drifted off to sleep.

Adriano awoke to the smell of smoke. He opened his eyes and saw Maria building a fire. It was still dark but you could feel the new day. An invisible sun set the clouds on the horizon alight, while birdsongs and the distant call of monkeys came from the forest. He lay there watching Maria as she moved about. She left a small container of water on the fire, slipped into the canoe, and quietly headed towards the lake, pulling hard on the paddles.

"It'll be a laugh if she goes off with my canoe," thought Adriano. "At least my shotgun and knife stayed here." But she wouldn't do that. She had nowhere to go. And anyway, she'd left her paltry little bundle of things by the fire.

Maria was back half an hour later with some leaves and herbs.

"My mother taught me how to make tea."

It was Adriano's first breakfast since the death of his father and his rushed departure from Lábrea, so far away now.

ΦΦΦ

It wasn't easy living together in the tiny canoe, which wasn't even ten feet long. Just changing clothes or taking care of bodily needs left them exposed and all the more embarrassed. They took turns steering, which unwittingly gave the traveling companion in the stern a splendid view. When it rained, their wet clothing left little to the imagination, and Adriano could see the outline of Maria's still small breasts. She was lanky, with shapely legs and long straight black hair that belied her ancestry, a mixture of native Brazilian with white European. She was a true dark-skinned *cabocla* but with dazzling green eyes. When she rowed, parts of her body

16

that were usually covered by her T-shirt or Adidas shorts would timidly peek out, and Adriano discovered the girl's skin tone was much lighter, that she'd actually been tanned by the relentless sun. Something else he soon realized was that his traveling companion knew a lot more about life in the jungle than he did. He was amazed that her senses were so much sharper than his and that she was enviably accurate in reading the mysterious sounds of the forest.

Four days after they had fled Lake Igapó-Mirim, their canoe reached the region of Surara, one of the most beautiful lakes in the Amazon. They needed to rest for a few days and this would be a good place. The lake wasn't inhabited but there was a small village next to the narrow entrance, on the right bank of the Purus. Maria was mesmerized by the endless comings and goings of canoes equipped with small, makeshift motors, which the *caboclos* used for fishing and transportation. On Igapó-Mirim, she'd seen fishing boats with big motors off in the distance, even a few yachts and canoes equipped with commercial outboard motors. Her stepfather had sometimes hired out as a guide for the fishermen, but he'd done his best to keep his family well away from the visitors. That's how he brought in a little cash to buy coffee, sugar, *cachaça*, salt, and even some clothes from the traveling merchants who stopped by the lake once or twice a year looking to buy Brazil nuts, copaiba oil, dry pirarucu, and turtles and tortoises.

17

In Surara, Maria had contact with strangers for the first time in her life and saw some of the wonders of civilization. The floating rigs that were always at anchor near the village held a tad of everything. The most remarkable thing was without a doubt the radio, which never stopped talking or playing music or announcing the news. Before then, the only music young Maria had ever heard was her mother's mumbled singing. Like the music, almost everything in this universe was novel, astounding, and captivating. Adriano watched the awakening of the timid girl from Lake Igapó-Mirim with a mixture of tenderness and compassion. She looked like a frightened yet curious little creature who couldn't hide her overpowering interest and delight in getting to know this wonderful, intriguing new world.

None of what Maria was coming into contact with for the first time was new to Adriano. In Lábrea, he'd led the typical life of someone in a small town of the Amazon interior. He'd gone to school, learned to read, write, and do math, played a lot of soccer with his friends, experienced his first crushes, and, more recently, had experimented sexually with some ardent neighbors and eager classmates. Tall, strong, and good-looking, he was used to making a hit with the women. His father Renildo worked at the Banco do Brasil, a large public-owned bank. He owned his own home and had accumulated a few more possessions than the average resident of the small town, where a family's prosperity was measured by the number of mosquito nets it had.

When Adriano was 15, his mother died following a sudden, ruthless illness that the town doctor hadn't been able to identify. It wasn't long before his father, an attractive young widower, had found comfort in the arms of a much younger woman. He remarried and the four sons from his first marriage were quickly joined by new offspring. Adriano's older brothers lost no time moving out, partly because their stepmother, who was about their age, was not easy to take. One of them was lucky enough to get a job at City Hall and the other two enlisted in the Army. Adriano, the youngest and still in his last year of school, was the only one to stay in their father's house. He was his father's favorite, the one he'd take fishing and hunting on the weekends. Renildo knew he was about to get a promotion and nice raise, so he decided to invest in his favorite pastime by having a new, more comfortable canoe built. There was a crude shipyard not far from their house and almost every day after work at the bank, Renildo would wile away an hour or so watching the handiwork progress. During a visit to the shipyard, a heavy wooden beam came loose from a large ship and its full weight fell squarely on top of him. The former future personal manager at the Banco do Brasil branch in Lábrea died on the spot, and so fast he had no time to feel pain. All indications were that someone's negligence had caused the unfortunate tragedy, with no ill intent. Since there was no interest in investigating the case, and the witnesses claimed they hadn't seen anything at all, the person responsible was never identified. And that was that, as far as Renildo's death was concerned.

Once Adriano had gotten over the shock, he realized that without his father around, he was a stranger in the family. No doubt about it, it was time to go. Anticipating the inevitable surfacing of quarrels and misunderstandings with his father's young widow, Adriano was quick to suggest dividing the deceased's estate in a way that was highly advantageous to her. He'd sell the old canoe and keep the new one, along with the shotgun, one mosquito netting, some old family photos, and all of his father's fishing gear. His stepmother would get the house and everything in it, as well as his father's Banco do Brasil pension. Since the young woman had no interest in canoes, shotguns, casting nets, or bait and hooks, she immediately accepted the offer.

Adriano stayed on in the house for a few more days while he sold the old canoe. The pittance he got for it was barely enough to cover his father's debt to the shipyard, but the owner, who felt a touch of guilt, refused to accept payment. So with a bit of money in his pocket and a brand-new canoe, Adriano said his farewells at last. He'd already made up his mind: he'd travel down the Purus River and then the Solimões to the city of Manaus.

ΦΦΦ

Fewer than fifty families lived in Surara, so it proved a fine place for Maria to tackle the long learning curve demanded by her new life. Adriano made friends in just a few days and managed to get permission from the community leader to take shelter in what remained of an old houseboat, the only one anchored inside the lake. The next step was to go hunting, and the region was thick with ducks, tapirs, and deer. Meanwhile, Maria spent the days on Dona Neide's houseboat, a general-store-cum-restaurant-cum-meeting place. The girl began by helping the proprietor out in the kitchen, where she learned to cook. She was soon skilled at making dishes from all types of fish—sardines, tambaqui, pirarucu, flagtail. She could even fix a mean catfish stew.

The two of them spent less time together now, because Adriano left early and sometimes spent the whole day and night out fishing and hunting. The untouched woodlands climbing high hills around Lake Surara were famous for their enormous trees, hundreds of years old. The forests were home to a broad diversity of animals while the crystal-clear waters held fish to please all palates. Adriano made a little money with his fishing and even more on game. He used the income to patch up the roof a bit, making the hut much more livable. With a bigger area protected from the rain, now he wouldn't need to sleep under Maria's hammock, which was protected by the tarp.

On weekends, Dona Neide's floating rig turned into a nightclub. A small Honda generator produced enough electricity for a little lighting and also ran a refrigerator and freezer, filled to the brim with beer for the thirsty fishermen. On Saturdays, a large boat came in from the town of Manacapuru loaded with ice, soda, beer, *cachaça*, as well as a number of young ladies who were always up for engaging in small talk, sipping a few cold ones, dancing, and even relieving the stress of the more generous fishermen. These "working women" (they were too old to be called girls) were no longer able to compete on the cutthroat market in Manacapuru—the biggest city around at a population of over 30,000.

A JVC sound system that the *caboclos* called a three-in-one—radio, record player, and cassette—guaranteed lots of unbridled fun for everyone. Once the first cans of beers and shots of *cachaça* had been thrown back, the music was turned up got louder, spirits got happier, the dancing started, and so did the inevitable cheek-to-cheek on and off the dance floor. Not unpredictably, the parties often ended in a brawl or even gunfire. Dona Neide wanted none of that on her houseboat; she just wanted to sell eats and drinks. Any troublemakers were quickly invited to leave and the meanest told never to come back.

For Maria, these crowds were a matchless opportunity. Until she took over the cooking, the customers had always ordered something to eat early in the evening and then stuck strictly to drinks. The kitchen in fact closed up early. But after she had a year's worth of experience under her belt, Maria felt confident enough to insist that Dona Neide extend the hours and add fried fish sticks, boiled manioc, purple yam, and other Amazonian delicacies to the menu for the starving merry-makers. The idea proved a great hit.

Thrilled to see the extra money coming in, Dona Neide started paying her new cook a little better. Maria could thus afford her first sodas and taste some beer—which she rejected, even ice cold. She bought some new clothes, because the skinny little girl had matured quickly and outgrown her former kid's clothing. Much to Adriano's surprise, the Adidas shorts were traded in for feminine outfits, and suddenly the girl he'd been introducing as his sister had transformed into an attractive woman that men couldn't keep their eyes off. Maria eventually became the central attraction on Dona Neide's houseboat. Whenever they ordered food, some of the more audacious fishermen—even including friends of Adriano's—pushed their way into the kitchen to talk to her. It was almost always to ask her to dance or invite her out the next day. Despite her refusals, the horde of admirers kept on growing, and the reputation of the pretty green-eyed *cabocla* with firm thighs and an unpopped cherry drew fishermen that had never before set foot on Dona Neide's houseboat.

Her sudden renown began to be a bother. Maria couldn't be left alone for a minute anymore without protection. The decrepit houseboat that sheltered them was anchored in an isolated spot, and so Adriano went out hunting at night less and less. It was even dangerous to leave her alone in the daytime. Canoes would float right by the houseboat ever so slowly, as if by happen-

stance, curious eyes hungering for a glimpse of its lovely occupant. When Adriano and Maria had arrived in
Surara a year before, nobody had paid heed to the girl,
but a radical change had clearly taken place. Whenever
some randy fellow came round, full of flattery and
sweet talk, Adriano found himself overwhelmed by a
strange sensation, totally new to him. What was worse,
Maria seemed to like the whole show. As she walked
away, she'd treat her admirers to a swing of her hips
that took your breath away.

"When I finish paying off my clothes, I'm going to
buy you a new hammock," she promised Adriano one
day.

"The hammock we've got is big enough for both of
us, if you weren't so stubborn," he thought, but he said
nothing. He most assuredly did not want a hammock to
himself.

Adriano couldn't bear to think of the day when Maria would take a liking to the countless come-ons, but he
was well aware the time would come. The idea pained
him.

ΦΦΦ

Early one morning as the first sunbeams peeked timidly into the houseboat, Adriano noticed that Maria's
hammock was empty. Where could she have gone? That
strange sensation tugged at his insides. He got up and
looked outside. The sun wasn't completely up, and a

light fog shrouded the lake. His breath caught in his throat. Next to the houseboat, the water around her knees, Maria was taking a bath, naked from the waist up. Not even during the week they'd spent together in the canoe, paddling down to Surara, had he seen her so bare. Back then she'd looked like a boy ready to play soccer. She had had nothing in common with the female he was seeing now. From where he was, he could savor the sight of her slender figure and white breasts, a contrast with her round pointed nipples and the rest of her body, toasted by the sun. A strong sensation swept over him, and he didn't need to look down to know his excitement was quite visible. As Maria started to turn towards the houseboat, Adriano ducked inside. When she came in later, dressed, she found him sitting on the floor and stretching, as if he'd just woken up.

"Good morning! You slept in."

"I'm going to clean my shotgun today and take care of some stuff around the house," he replied, as if nothing had happened.

"I'm going to spend the day here too. I need to wash clothes."

They did chores all morning. When the noonday heat arrived, they sought shade in the airiest corner of the houseboat to wait for the sun to ease off a bit. Even the dolphins looked for cooler waters at that hour of the day.

"Tell me something about your life," Maria said. "The only thing I know is that you're from Lábrea and you're an orphan."

"Nothing much of interest to tell. School, family, brothers. Then my mother died." The words came out hard at first, but the thought of his mother spurred other memories. He talked about the happy days of his child-hood, at school, and about his father's recent death. Then he remembered a funny incident that had taken place during his earliest days on the Purus River and he burst out laughing.

"Tell me! What are you thinking about?" Maria wanted to join in his mirth.

One week before reaching Lake Igapó-Mirim, Adri-ano explained, he had stopped by another lake, equally isolated. It wasn't long before he'd found a houseboat with a number of canoes anchored out front and not a soul in sight. He'd rowed up close and clapped his hands, as strangers did when they wanted to announce their presence. He heard low voices inside the house but no one came out. So he tied his canoe up to the floating platform and knocked on the door. In the shadows he could make out several folks around a hammock, where an old man was lying, half naked.

"Praise God!" the old man mumbled when he saw the silhouette in the doorway. "The priest has come!"

The men around the hammock quickly explained what was going on. Their father was dying and, as a man of faith, he'd asked for the priest. It had been two days since the youngest son had headed off to the near-est parish. The old man no longer recognized anyone, and still the priest hadn't appeared. He lived a good stretch away, and maybe the messenger hadn't found him—a lot might have happened. But none of that mattered anymore! The stranger who had stumbled in could easily pass for the priest. The old man had reached the end and he wouldn't know any better. And so Adriano was forced to spend most of the night holding a dying man's hand, until the old fellow kicked the bucket, just before dawn.

Maria couldn't stop laughing. She was more than familiar with the peculiar, isolated life at those lost ends of the earth and she could easily imagine the scene. Those thoughts took her back to Lake Igapó-Mirim. She grew serious as she remembered her mother and her brothers and sisters. She was quiet for a few minutes and then she said, I don't know how to read or write. I'm ashamed. And I don't have my papers; I was never registered—I practically don't exist."

"We'll register you in Manacapuru. Surara doesn't have a notary public or a police station. Maybe I can teach you to read and write. I'll see if I can dig up a notebook, pencil, and maybe a textbook." Adriano liked the idea. They'd spend hours together, with him as the teacher.

Adriano woke up early the next day, as always, but he stayed where he was. He saw Maria get up and go out. He waited a bit and then followed her. Much to his delight, the scene from yesterday repeated itself, this time even better. The girl scooped up water with a gourd and poured it over her long hair, a look of pleas-

27

ure in her eyes. Adriano held his breath as he glimpsed her for a few moments with nothing to hide her skin. She had a young girl's perfect body, proud breasts and prominent nipples, a thin waist, firm buttocks, and a sharply defined triangle of pubic hair. As soon as she started to get dressed, he rushed back to his spot on the ground and lay down again. He was so beside himself with desire that it actually hurt. He stayed there without moving for a while, until his erection went away, and then he got up.

"I'm late," he exclaimed, and he hurried to the canoe. He paddled furiously away, like a madman.

ΦΦΦ

The next two days—Friday and Saturday—were especially busy, so Maria stayed overnight on Dona Neide's houseboat. It was also duck hunting season, something Adriano couldn't miss out on. As he lay in his canoe Friday night, sleep evaded him. He couldn't get Maria out of his head. He'd never felt anything like it before. Thinking about her made him happy, anxious, and even a tad dizzy. Her smile, her eyes, her hair, her breasts, the sway of her firm behind, her defiant ways, her mere presence—it all mesmerized him. It was hard to believe she'd grown up all at once, right there beside him, and he hadn't even noticed these fine qualities. He gradually came to recognize that he was madly in love—and afraid of losing her. He needed to deal with this dilemma, and as soon as possible. Cradled by these thoughts, sleep finally came over him.

When the weekend was over, Adriano picked Maria up at Dona Neide's and they went back home together. Adriano had intended to waste no time declaring his love, but the words got stuck in his throat. They went to sleep as always, each in a different spot, her in the hammock and him on the floor. He woke before the first rays of dawn but pretended he was still asleep, until he saw Maria leave her hammock and head outside. It was a replay of the other days. Excited and impatient, he waited a bit and then went out after her, like before. He was perplexed when he didn't find her in the usual place. He edged closer to the water, puzzled, but still he couldn't see her. Starting to get worried, he headed over to the other side of the houseboat, where the water was deep enough to swim. Suddenly, he felt a blow that caused him to lose his balance and topple into the water. Before he went under, he realized Maria had pushed him—and was coming in too. Still dazed, he found his footing in the waist-high water. Without a single word, Maria wrapped herself around him, hard.

He felt her breasts graze against his chest as her thighs hugged him hungrily and her greedy mouth sucked on his lips. Melded into each other, they rose out of the water. He started kissing her ears and neck, moving down to her nipples, while he filled his hands with her curved buttocks. Only then did he realize she was completely naked. He felt her body tremble as her nipples grew hard and her legs squeezed him tighter. He carried her out of the water. As soon as their feet touched the sand, she pulled him hard, until he fell gently on top of her. He eagerly sought her breasts again, and then slid his hand downward until he touched her triangle of coarse hair and felt the blood pulsing beneath. His mouth crept to her naval and then back up to kiss her budding breasts. Her body shuddered in response to his caresses. She stroked him through his shorts and then thrust her hand inside, her movement swift and sure. Now it was Adriano who shivered. He yanked off his shorts. Possessed by desire, he crushed her body with the weight of his, while Maria held him as delicately, sensitively, and precisely as a violinist holds his bow. Excited and impatient, she guided him inside her.

The act was slow. Maria was tense at first, but in a few moments she relaxed and embraced him again with her thighs, their bodies united in a soft rhythmic movement. And then she murmured something incomprehensible. The sound filled his head and drove him over the edge. He felt his body contract in a deliciously painful spasm that was more intense than anything he'd ever imagined.

Afterwards, they lay side by side on the ground, trying to catch their breath. Maria kissed him again and whispered, "I'm not going to buy a new hammock anymore." They burst out laughing.

Then she confessed. "Last week you spied on me when I was taking a bath. I saw you. I took everything off on purpose, to see what you'd do—but nothing happened. Looked to me like you got scared."

A little while later, Maria nestled back into his arms and climbed playfully onto his belly. She bent over to bite his ear and then traveled down his neck, sucking on him until he felt an odd tickling that gave him goosebumps all over. Leisurely she brought her small, firm breasts to his mouth and offered them up. He bit one nipple and then the other, until they once again grew turgid with desire.

"We have to make up for lost time," he thought as he felt his desire and his strength return.

"You took forever to see me," she mumbled.

ΦΦΦ

They stayed in Surara only two more months. As fate would have it, they ended up going straight to Manaus without stopping in Manacapuru. It so happened that the *Igaratim-Açu*, a large passenger boat, dropped anchor at the mouth of the lake and the captain was looking for a good guide who could take the big boss out fishing by canoe. Adriano offered his services. They brought in a good catch and, at the end of the day, he was invited to have dinner with the crew. While they were shooting the breeze, Adriano picked up some valuable information, the frosting on his sizeable earnings for the day: the boat was in urgent need of a cook and another crew member. The next day, Maria did a trial

31

run in the *Igaratim-Açu*'s kitchen. Her cooking was such a hit that Adriano didn't even have to prove his own skills. Hired on the spot, the couple loaded up their belongings, said goodbye to Dona Neide and their other neighbors, and set sail for Manaus.

The trip and all that followed was a new experience not just for Maria but for Adriano as well. The Solimões River was bigger and mightier than any they'd seen before. In a few brief hours, the great river's swift current, aided by the ship's powerful engines, had carried the *Igaratim-Açu* to the majestic meeting of the muddy waters of the Solimões with the dark, calm waters of the Negro River. It took their breath away. The two giant rivers ran side by side for miles on end, their waters never mixing, until finally, weary of battling it out, they merged into one to form the almighty Amazon. It was a spectacular show.

"I'd heard about it, but I never could have imagined it!" Adriano exclaimed. Nestled in his arms as if seeking protection from some overpowering force, a solemn-faced Maria watched it all with a mixture of awe and wonder. The rest of the crew understood what the two young people were feeling. They'd all felt something similar when they'd first seen that overwhelming force of nature.

The sound of a siren pierced the air as the *Igaratim-Açu* sailed by a cargo ship laden with a mountain of iron ore. As they approached the port, they crossed paths with another ship, this one even bigger.

"These are the little ships," the captain explained. "Manaus has a population of around 300,000 and it's not even a big city. Brazil has a lot of cities much bigger."

Their first days in Manaus were crammed with new experiences. Maria and Adriano lived on the *Igaratim-Açu*, where they did cleaning and maintenance work. Most of the crew, except for Captain Pedrinho, were temporary employees and were rarely around when the ship was docked. Adriano and Maria had lots of free time and he took the opportunity to start teaching Maria how to read and write. She proved an excellent student and was soon devouring every newspaper that showed up on the vessel, even older editions and ones that had been used as wrapping. There was a broad assortment of news stories. Those were turbulent times, on the eve of Brazil's 1964 military coup.

The months they had spent as apprentices aboard the *Igaratim-Açu* made their adaptation to the big city all that much easier. They acquired experience and learned how to fit in to the new world unfolding before them. Their contact with the occupants of other boats anchored in the stream by Educandos was essential to helping them grow to understand life in Manaus and Brazil. True, only on the weekends did they have enough time to really tour the city and take in its sights. They strolled through the Praça da Matriz and down Eduardo Ribeiro Avenue, went to the movies at Cine Politeama, had ice-cream at Leiteria Amazonas, and drank coffee at Bar Americano. Maria was so taken with cinema that she couldn't sleep for several nights after a Hitchcock film and went around with a huge grin on her face for a week after a good comedy starring Oscarito.

In the 1960s, Manaus was a city in decay. It had enjoyed prosperity during the early twentieth-century rubber boom and had inherited the infrastructure left behind by the British, worn but still working. The architectural highlight was the large number of Portuguese mansions with their high ceilings and enormous windows—the secret to good ventilation. Imposing buildings and structures like the Palace of Justice, the Municipal Market, the customs house and port, the governor's mansion—called Rio Negro Palace—and the Teatro Amazonas opera house served as an insistent reminder to unapprised visitors that the city had known much better days. Downtown streets were paved and the abundance of trees offered some relief from the heat. What was bothersome, however, was the sluggish economy and joblessness. Albeit very poorly paid, Maria and Adriano were very lucky to have work.

But their luck was short-lived. As to be expected, their superbly delightful hours of cavorting, mischief-making, cuddling, laughter, and moans in the hammock bore fruit. One fine day Maria felt odd, threw up, and then slept for several hours. Over the coming weeks, she continued to vomit, her breasts grew larger, her bouts of nausea and sleepiness more frequent, and her period stopped. She was clearly pregnant. Bursting with pride and not really aware of the implications of this fact, they told Captain Pedrinho. He raised his eyebrows.

"She can't stay on the boat with a baby," he announced.

Much as the captain regretted having to do it, he advised Adriano to look for a new place to live and work. Captain Pedrinho was a good man. He felt sorry for the young couple, knowing how hard it would be for them to find work, but he couldn't go against the rules set by the vessel's owner. Chagrined, he decided to give them sixty days to get their affairs sorted out. It was the best he could do.

Only then did Adriano and Maria begin to understand the seriousness of their situation. Apparently things had changed. News from the south told of a divided country, which was arguing over the failure of some businesses to invest and the thievery of others, and about how it was time to face the music on the political scene. On March 31, 1964, the Armed Forces had seized power and promised to put the house in order, but things didn't seem to be headed in that direction. Groups formed to fight the dictatorship. The situation was very unstable in Manaus as well. But what worried the couple most was the fear that their child would be born before they'd settled the problem of Maria's papers. They refused to let their child be born into the same messy situation.

Captain Pedrinho was still feeling bad about firing them, and he figured he might help by introducing them to an attorney he knew, one who often leased the *Igaratim-Açu*. The lawyer needed a good cook for his daughter's birthday party, and Maria saw this as a chance to win the favor and assistance of a powerful man, so she cooked up a storm. The lawyer's wife, a kind-hearted woman, was moved by the young girl's story. She spoke to her husband and his influential friends about it. And so it was that just a few days later, the young couple had a birth certificate proving that Maria B. Brasil had been born in Santarém, Pará, on January 14, 1948. Nobody knew where the document came from or what the "B" stood for or why her last name was Brasil, nor was there any explanation for the choice of date or birthplace. What mattered was that Maria now existed and even had the mandatory government-issued ID card.

Meanwhile, an ad in the newspaper *A Crítica* caught Adriano's eye. Someone was looking for a groundskeeper to tend to a *banho*—a weekend property on the edge of the city, crisscrossed by the crystal-clear waters of idyllic streams, where its owners could seek relief from the muggy days of an equatorial summer. It would be a good way to get a job, with housing to boot. That was how Adriano made the acquaintance of Benjamin Melul, who was getting ready to spend some time living in the rubber forests of Quatro Ases. In the early twentieth century, Brazil's rubber forests had produced tremendous amounts of latex and had sustained the Melul family for many years. Benjamin was convinced that the huge piece of fertile property on the distant Abunã River, bordering Bolivia, could be productive again and generate wealth for the Melul family. It was worth a try. During his absence, he'd need someone to take care of his family's property, a well-located *banho* and his mansion in downtown Manaus. The men's meeting was a success. Benjamin took an immediate liking to the personable Adriano. He was struck by the story of Adriano and his young girlfriend in the forests of the Purus River. The arrangement seemed perfect, and Adriano agreed to think it over.

The next day, Adriano and Maria presented themselves at the Melul family's mansion, where they had a lengthy conversation with Benjamin and his wife Nina. They soon closed a deal that seemed to be to everyone's advantage. The Meluls couldn't afford to pay much but the *banho* was big and had an abundance of fruit trees. The couple could raise some chickens, plant some manioc, and their survival would be assured. Moreover, the baby that was due in a few months would have a home.

But later that night, Nina suggested something else to her husband: "Why don't we take them with us to Quatro Ases? I'd feel safer. They've got a gun and lots of experience in the woods—just what we don't have. Adriano seems like a sensible young man and Maria seems like a nice, hard-working *cabocla* too. We can't pay them but we can offer them a share of the profits.

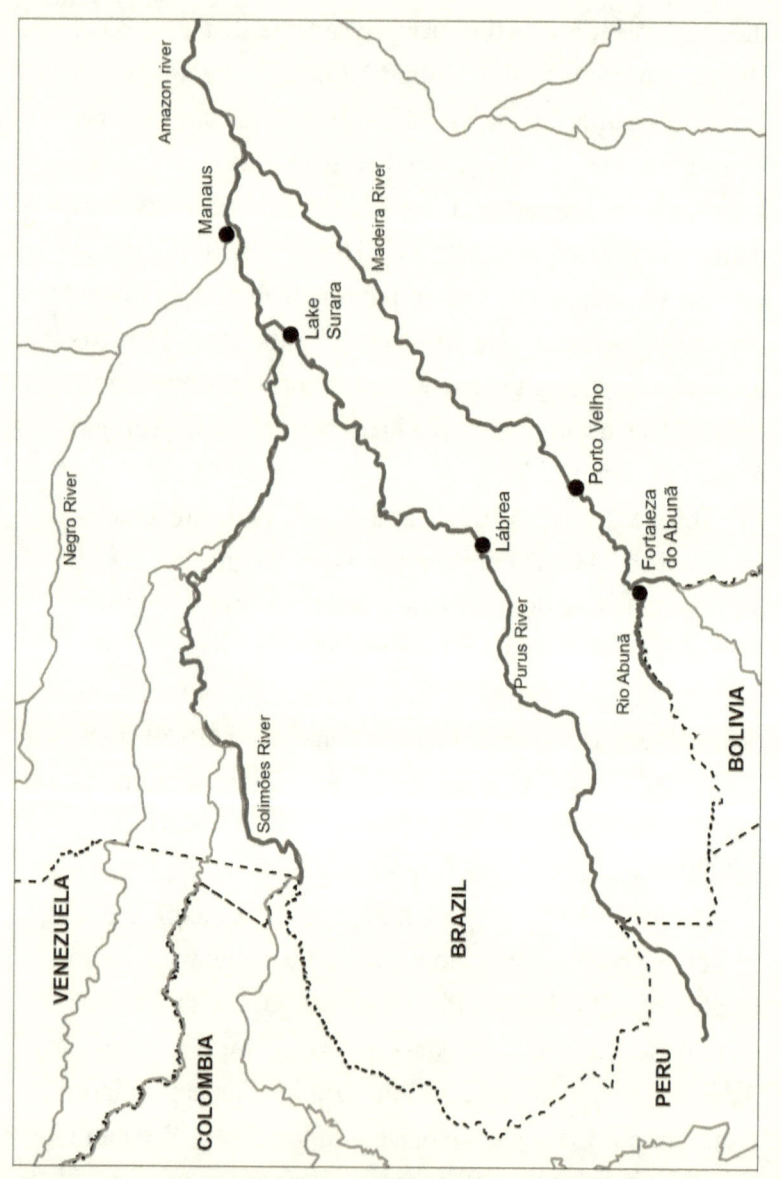

Twenty percent should make them quite happy, and we'd be safer. Our only up-front expense would be the tickets to Porto Velho and Fortaleza do Abunã. There are plenty of candidates to take care of our *banho* in Manaus."

ΦΦΦ

One month later, the two couples embarked for Porto Velho outfitted with everything imaginable. You can't forget anything when you head off to the rubber-tapping region, things like weapons, ammunition, matches, knives and hatchets, cloth, needle and thread, pots and pans, sturdy shoes, hats, hammocks and mosquito netting, salt, coffee, sugar, a calendar, and even books.

By the time the boat finally made dock a little ways from the gigantic Fortaleza do Abunã waterfall—the point at which the river became unnavigable—Maria's pregnancy was quite visible but she still radiated happiness and a readiness to work.

Getting from the river to the rubber groves was no picnic. Their rented wagon squeezed its way along the narrow dirt road that had been cut through the forest many years earlier. The forest was so overgrown that the road had shrunk to a trail and in some spots they had to blaze through, chopping off branches and felling small trees. In the township of Fortaleza do Abunã, Benjamin hired another two experienced rubber tappers, promising each of them ten percent of the yield.

The small group had to spend two nights in the forest before they reached their clearing, now practically consumed by secondary forest. There, in the shade of a giant ceiba tree, stood the abandoned headquarters, where the big boss used to live. Part of the wooden building remained standing, but the floor and roof were in deplorable shape. Much of the timber had rotted away and had to be replaced. It took nearly two months to make the place habitable and clean up the surrounding area. The rubber tappers' homes stood in a smaller clearing a ways off, hidden in the shadow of some trees. These buildings were in worse shape yet, but after much work the new occupants managed to restore two of them.

During their long days of toil and of no comfort at all, Nina and Maria forged a friendship. Nina thanked her lucky stars that she had this strong *cabocla* to rely on; she admired Maria's amazing joy, hard work, and prodigious knowledge of the forest. Maria, on the other hand, appreciated the courage, kindness, and common sense that Nina always had at the ready. Now, with the help of Nina, her Portuguese grammar improved and she even picked up a little math. Maria reciprocated by sharing her practical knowledge: she showed Nina how to survive without a maid, cleaning house and making the meals herself; how to interpret the sounds of the forest; and how to cope with adversity with the ease and acceptance of a *cabocla*. It was during these hard but hopeful times that Maria got her nickname. When Nina saw "Maria B. Brasil" printed on the girl's ID card, she said, "But of course! 'B' for Bonita—pretty!" And the name stuck.

After a two-month period of adaptation, Quatro Ases finally produced its first *pelas*—giant balls of rubber. And none too soon because Benjamin's savings had run out. They quickly discovered the rubber lands weren't very profitable. Production costs were high, latex prices extremely low, shipping distances far, and profit almost nil.

In the midst of all this, Isaías was born, a big, healthy, lovable glutton with strong lungs and his mother's green eyes. One year later, Nina and Benjamin had Alice. The next year came Isaías' sister, Lídia, and then little Ariel, Alice's brother. When the contracted tappers gave up after nearly five years without showing profit, Benjamin and Adriano still stuck with it. When they too eventually admitted that their experiment was a failure, all that remained to do was gather strength for the return to Manaus. The time had come to return to blessed civilization.

CHAPTER 2
QUATRO ASES

The sky was heavy with black clouds and the wind brought the strong scent of rain, warning that another Amazonian deluge was falling somewhere and would soon be upon them. Benjamin had to cross the river before the dark of night fell and, more importantly, before the storm hit. The canoe was tied to the trunk of a small bush on the Bolivian side, right where the clear waters of the Abunã met the dark waters of a tiny branch that flowed out of the Bolivian highlands, cleaving the wild, dense virgin forest that covered those far ends of the earth.

The Abunã isn't very wide and it wasn't going to take more than a few minutes to cross over to Brazil. Most of the work had already been done. Only four *pelas* of rubber still sat atop the riverbank. Benjamin just had to load them and then he could leave while it was still quite light out. He was beginning yet another huff-and-puff trudge up the bank when the rain began to fall. At almost the same time, the forest was pierced by a fearsome thundering noise that came from the smaller river. It sounded like a runaway train hurtling towards him. He had just turned around when he saw a huge wave practically the height of a man surging violently into the calm waters of the Abunã—a wall of water ripping trees out by their roots and laying waste to all in its path. He didn't even notice when the raging waters swallowed his frail canoe of precious rubber like some tiny toy.

Benjamin knew exactly what had just happened. Much earlier, at the very outset of their time in the region, he had witnessed the damage done by this same rare phenomenon. That day, a torrential rain had fallen upstream. In a short space of time, the sky dumped a veritable monsoon at the headwaters. There, trunks of toppled trees clogged the riverbed while seaweed and other organic waste plugged up any holes, forming a natural dam that held the rainwater in. With hardly anything seeping past this dam, the waters backed up and gave birth to a temporary lake. As more rain hammered down, the natural weir eventually gave way and a booming explosion of water carried off all obstacles in its path as it roared violently downstream in a terrifying force of nature. The wall of water tore up trees, destroyed houseboats, breeched the riverbanks to wipe out homes, and dragged pieces of its damage along with it. Nothing could withstand its brutal strength.

That first time, Benjamin had gotten off light, suffering little damage. But this time the destruction was complete. The raging waters not only crushed his boat; they also swallowed up his six precious *pelas*, the fruit of so many years of labor. The *pelas* represented the salvation of the Melul family and their coveted return to civilization, where they'd at least have neighbors to talk to, school for their children, medical care, a synagogue to attend on the Sabbath, and a movie theater to go to on Sundays. He knew Nina had decided she was going to return to Manaus with the children whether he went or not. Right at that moment, she was alone in the main house on the Brazilian side, anxiously waiting his return. The old building of rotting wood had known better days, days of prosperity and power, but now it was simply falling apart. In a little while, Ariel and Alice would be asleep while Nina would be awake in the dark, counting the minutes until Benjamin got home, listening to the mysterious sounds of the forest and dreaming about their impending return to the big city.

Brokenhearted and exhausted, Benjamin looked for a flat spot with a little shelter from the rain and prepared himself to spend a long night. Luckily his hatchet hadn't been in the canoe and that gave him some sense of security. The waters had taken his shotgun and matches, but still, he wasn't completely defenseless. In a dense forest, night is always pitch black and strange sounds intrude from all directions, sometimes terrifying and threatening. Most people would find themselves petrified with fear but not Benjamin, who was by then a fairly experienced woodsman.

Even though he was tired, he tried to stay awake and protect himself from the mosquitoes. He said some prayers and then, soothed by sleepiness and fatigue, drifted back to his childhood at Dom Pedro II Public

High School in faraway Manaus. At the very least, he had to provide Alice and Ariel with an education. The thought seemed to restore his energies. Yes, he was going to get back on his feet! There were still twelve *pelas* on the Brazilian side, a small harvest of Brazil nuts, and—most importantly—he, Nina, and the children were alive. The *caboclo* Adriano was strong and experienced and, with his help, they'd be able to get back to the city and start their lives over again. Things could have been much worse.

Nina had been entirely right to rebel. It was high time to admit that the young couple's return to the Melul family rubber groves on the Abunã River had been an utter failure. Not even the area's magnificent waterfalls and white-sand beaches had made it worth it.

Benjamin's grandfather had bought Quatro Ases in the early twentieth century, and for a while he had prospered. True, he lived a little beyond the ends of the earth but, on the other hand, he produced a great deal of latex. As a very successful rubber baron, his grandfather had earned a great deal of money fast and had become one of the richest people in Manaus. With the sad end of the first Rubber Battle in 1915—after cheap, plentiful Malaysian latex had conquered the world market and Brazil's customers had disappeared—the well had gone dry and his family had lost almost everything acquired during the boom. His nine grandchildren were left with a decrepit old mansion in downtown Manaus, a *banho*, and the far-off Quatro Ases rubber groves, abandoned for many years. None of this was worth much anymore, but the memory of those years of prosperity remained alive and the story of Grandpa Melul was told over and over again by the now destitute family.

In the early 1960s, the Melul family scattered to more thriving places, like Rio de Janeiro and São Paulo. Only the newlywed Benjamin and Nina found themselves captivated by their ancestor's spirit of adventure and by the dream of reviving the golden days. And so off they set to spend a period in that remote, virgin land on the border with Bolivia. They hoped to make some money selling rubber and other regional products while they explored the area's untamed beauty. From what Benjamin had heard from his grandfather, a young, love-struck couple like them wouldn't even miss their friends or relatives in that isolated corner of Brazil.

ΦΦΦ

Weary to his bones but cradled by his memories, Benjamin fell into the light sleep of a wild animal, all senses on alert. In the wee hours of the night, somewhere nearby, a massive tree weakened by the deluge, or perhaps simply very old, crashed to the ground, crushing the vegetation around it. Surrounded by darkness, Benjamin didn't even have time to pray when the deafening sound came. Silence returned at once, disturbed only by the noises of the woods settling into a new position. It was the forest renewing itself as it had for thousands of years. With the first rays of dawn, the mosquitoes returned, along with Benjamin's awareness that he had escaped by a hair.

"My time hadn't come," he sighed in relief. "I hope I don't get malaria again."

He couldn't get back to sleep and as he waited for the sun to rise, he went back to remembering the early days in the rubber groves. Old man Melul had warned his grandchildren that life in the forest was no picnic. He'd told them about the isolation and loneliness and how he didn't have a calendar so he'd calculated the Jewish holy days by the position of the moon. His story had sounded so romantic that nobody paid attention to the other details. Nobody seemed to remember that around that same time, in the long-ago year of 1930, many other rubber tappers had abandoned their properties and made desperate escapes. The forests weren't producing enough anymore to guarantee even a meager living, leaving nothing but snake bites, hunger, disease, and loneliness. The Amazon saw its darkest year in 1932, when the price of a metric ton of rubber crashed to 34 pounds sterling—a fraction of its production cost—taking down with it even the most well-established rubber producers on the Abunã River. Casting their stubbornness aside, the Melul family—along with the Abrahims, the Benchimols, and the Reis—threw in the towel and sought shelter in Manaus and Belém.

Nearly forty years later, the economy was not picking up and the outlook remained bleak. The young couple had realized that without the high economic yield of yesteryear, nothing would be left for them, no matter how little they spent on food and no matter that they lived in the old rubber headquarters. When they had been about to go back, early on in their second year there, Nina had gotten pregnant, just to complicate things, and so they had delayed their return. After Alice was born, planning got overlooked and Nina got pregnant again. The second pregnancy had been problematic and Ariel came prematurely. Nina felt the first signs of labor two months before schedule, when the couple was on the Bolivian side. Even though her water had already broken, Nina insisted they take her back over to the other bank—her child was going to be born Brazilian. The birth would also be easier there and Maria Bonita could help. The trip across was agony. In the canoe were Benjamin and an old Indian woman who Nina had practically dragged to the riverbank. She was quite far along in her labor and the Indian's presence was essential. Ariel was in a hurry and he was born on the beach—but on the side of the river his mother wanted so much.

Despite precautions, malaria had attacked the whole family. The mosquito netting that covered their beds was useless, as was the strategy of staying indoors during the most dangerous hours of the day.

Nina's daily routine was to do the household chores and take care of the children. Maria helped out. In the late afternoon, Nina went inside and spent the rest of the day bent over an old sewing machine, making shirts and denim slacks for the rubber tappers who lived in the area. She worked in the shadows of a kerosene lamp, their only lighting at night. This additional little income brought in the equivalent of nearly one *pela* a year. Adriano was Benjamin's helper and partner. Their hard toil ended only on Friday night when Shabbat arrived. As the woman of the house, Nina would light the candles and Benjamin would recite the Kiddush by heart. Then he would read some Sabbath prayers and after dinner finish off the evening with his favorite book, *Pirke Avot: Ethics of our Fathers.*

Despite their hard work, all that Benjamin and Adriano had managed to put together over five years were ten *pelas* of rubber on the Bolivian side and a little more on the Brazilian. They estimated this would be enough to buy boat tickets to Porto Velho and then to Manaus. There would be a bit left over to help get them through the first few months in the city, while they started their lives over. Their toil and self-imposed privation had come to little avail and Nina didn't want to wait a single minute longer.

"If you want to stay, go ahead, but I'm leaving and taking the children," she shot at him on the first occasion she'd ever rebelled. "My children are going to have a college education! Alice has to start school soon. If you really love us, you'll come with us."

Benjamin had agreed. They could wait no longer. The solitude and isolation weighed on them and it was obvious their prospects were far from bright. It was time to admit defeat and leave before the next bout of malaria.

"We'll all go. The time has come," Benjamin had said, much to Nina's relief.

ΦΦΦ

When the first rays of sun appeared, Benjamin went down to the edge of the Abunã, which seemed back to normal. The only signs of yesterday's flash flood were the fact that the waters were somewhat muddier and a bit higher than usual. He was on the right bank of the river, which curved leftward a little ways downstream. He held out some hope that the force of the water might have thrown a few things out of the canoe at the bend. He walked along the river, frightening off birds and curious iguanas as he slashed his way through with his hatchet. He finally found a Styrofoam box and one of his paddles lying about six feet above the riverbed. A spark of hope burned for a short while. But much as Benjamin rummaged about feverishly, he found nothing. Then he heard a whistle from the other side of the river.

"Over here!" he yelled as loud as he could. He grabbed the whistle around his neck and answered back. Soon he heard the shrill sound again, now a little closer.

He had been the one to introduce the blessed whistle some years earlier as a means of communication, and everyone had embraced the idea. It had to be Adriano, who lived near the main house and was the only one who still worked at Quatro Ases. Benjamin was saved. As he continued to whistle, he thought in relief about the future. Encouraging news had been coming from far-off Manaus, where a new Free Trade Zone seemed to be offering a road to prosperity.

ΦΦΦ

It wasn't long before a tall, thin, young man appeared on a small white-sand beach across the river. Benjamin hacked his way through the thick vegetation with his hatchet and the two men were soon in sight of each other.

"Adriano, pal! I lost my canoe, my gun, and six *pelas* in that flash flood that came down from Bolivia. Lucky enough we've got a few left. I was looking around now, thinking I might find some more stuff. Have you seen Nina?"

The wind was blowing hard from the other direction and Adriano couldn't make out what he was saying. Benjamin shouted his question again. Once the message finally became clear, Adriano yelled back, "She's the one who sounded the alarm. She was all upset when you didn't show up last night. I'll go back and calm her down, and try to find a canoe to save what's left of the rubber. It might take a while because the flood carried off a lot of canoes too."

Despite the distance between them and their troubles communicating, they managed to arrange for Benjamin to gather up all he could salvage and wait in the same spot for Adriano to come back.

Later that day, Benjamin heard another whistle and answered right back. He didn't see any canoe but soon noticed the movement of people across the river.

"I brought Nina and Ariel," shouted Adriano. "The canoe will have to wait till tomorrow. Can you swim across? I'll throw you a rope when you get close enough."

He didn't think twice. Nina was waiting for him. He left his hatchet and shoes beside the *pelas* and dove into the river. Though he hadn't eaten in many hours, he was tough and he swam with broad strokes. The current caught him about halfway across but it didn't drag him so far that he couldn't reach the place where they were waiting for him. Adriano tossed him a rope. A weary Benjamin grabbed hold and was pulled ashore. Only then did he see Nina, who was watching on. Soaking wet and out of breath, he embraced her and felt her warm tears against his shoulder.

"Baruch Hashem, thank God, you're alive! I don't know how I made it through the night. I thought the worst!"

"I lost the boat, my gun, and six *pelas*," he said in a low voice, almost a whisper.

"We were very lucky," she countered. "Better to lose your saddle than your horse. We'll get it all back soon enough and return to Manaus before the year is up."

"You're not going to get rid of this old horse any time soon!" Benjamin laughed in relief.

Then he heard Ariel's voice, and Nina explained, "Ariel came with me. Alice stayed with Maria, Isaías, and Lídia at Adriano's house."

They spent the night in each others' arms, trying to hide under a tarp from the mosquitoes. The fire burned all night, offering some protection against cougars and other wild beasts but also disturbing the peace of a band of noisy monkeys that wouldn't quit screaming.

The canoe arrived the next day. The rubber was brought over to the Brazilian side and then carried two by two to the main house, on the back of a donkey Benjamin had bought on a trip to Fortaleza do Abunã. Benjamin slept peacefully for the first time in many nights. Lying next to him, Nina savored the rhythmic breathing of the man she loved and gave thanks to God that the nightmare was over.

Three days later, Benjamin started feeling ill; his body ached all over and he spiked a fever. Adriano came down with the same symptoms and at first it looked like they'd contracted malaria yet again. Nina soon started showing symptoms and then little Ariel. The night on the beach had brought disaster. Maria had to tend to the four patients, along with Alice, Isaías, and Lídia.

They grew sicker fast. Their noses bled and they coughed up blood. Their fevers climbed and their bodies were soon covered with blue blotches. Maria was all too familiar with those signs. It wasn't malaria. She was horrified to recognize a much more dangerous malady from her childhood on the Purus River: the dread yellow fever. Years earlier, she and her mother had escaped unscathed, but many others living around them had not been as fortunate. She knew she could do nothing to help, just pray. She clung in despair to Adriano's hand, trying to lend him a little more strength and pass him a bit of her own life force.

By the time little Ariel stopped breathing, Benjamin's and Nina's skin and eyes had turned yellowish. They were barely conscious, yet they still kept vomiting up a foul-smelling black substance. A few hours later, Maria stood despondently by as Adriano, Benjamin, and Nina took their final breaths at almost the same instant. During those anxious hours, the children hadn't even cried, pain drying their tears. They could sense something terrible was happening but could not comprehend the extent of the tragedy. In the midst of her absolute misery, Maria had to put her own pain aside to devote herself to them, especially Alice.

"My mommy and daddy went to sleep and left me all alone," she finally whimpered after a long silence. Maria felt the child's pain to her core. She grew groggy and numb but then snapped out of it, and the nightmare came back, hitting even harder.

"We need to get out of here as fast as we can," thought Maria as the next dawn followed that hellish night. With the help of her six-year-old son Isaías, she dug four graves behind the small storage shed that held the sad rubber *pelas*. Her arms were accustomed to brutal labor but digging those shovels full of dirt demanded more than physical strength; it required a tremendous amount of inner stamina. She only managed to do it because there was no other alternative. It was impossible to understand and accept such tremendous misfortune. In one fell swoop, she had lost the people she loved most in the world. Worst of all she had lost Adriano, the man who had taken care of her when she was a young girl, as if he were a devoted, loving brother, and who was now father to her two children. Never again would she hear the laughter of that man who was always happy, kind, and caring, who was at the same time her friend, protector, and lover.

Indifferent to the dramatic events of the night, the sun had made an especially spectacular show as it rose over the Abunã. Its rays bathed the imposing forest around the main house in glorious color. It was nearly time for the bugs to come out and thus to seek protection under mosquito netting. The only valuables that remained at the house were the *pelas*, mosquito netting, half a dozen chickens, and the donkey. Maria was afraid to leave the rubber unguarded in Quatro Ases. Without a cart, the donkey could carry two or maybe three balls at most, while she could walk with the children. On the one hand, she didn't want to leave the latex behind, since it was really her only asset. On the other, she knew she couldn't stay there much longer. The most feasible solution was to leave with the children and take as much latex as she could to Fortaleza do Abunã and then find help to go back and pick up the other *pelas*, which she'd need to hide somewhere. The next day she found two hiding spots in opposite directions, hoping she wouldn't risk losing them all if someone happened to stumble upon one of the stashes before her return. With the donkey's help, she began stowing them away, planning to move them two by two. The children went along in silence. Isaías even tried to help but the *pelas* got the better of him. After all, they weighed over a hundred pounds each and he couldn't even roll them.

When she got back from hiding the first two, Maria heard barking. It was Tata, the mutt Nina had raised. She looked around to see what was upsetting the dog, and that's when she caught sight of a cart in front of the main house. The next instant two men came out the front door, which she had left unlocked. It had been ages since the building had any windows and there wouldn't be any point in locking the door. She didn't know if the arrival of these two strangers was more a sign of great luck or of coming disaster. She wasn't happy that they had just barged right into an inhabited house, but there wasn't anything she could do about it. She tried to hide her anxiousness and called out a hello.

"Good afternoon, ma'am! We're stopping around here looking to buy hides, rubber, copaiba balsam, anything worthwhile. We saw you got some *pelas* for sale. Where's the man of the house?" the older of the two asked. Maria saw he had hardly any teeth.

They'd obviously gone through the place and found some of the latex, but they evidently hadn't noticed the graves behind the house.

"He should be home any time now," she replied, her fear growing. It was odd that their cart was nearly empty. The rare merchants who passed through always came laden with the goods they had purchased along the way, together with the coffee, salt, and sugar that served as barter.

"I think our boss Benjamin already has a customer for these *pelas*," she said, hoping against hope that the men would leave soon.

Maria had just turned 21 and even after the birth of two children, she was shapely and attractive. Nina had gotten in the habit of calling her Professor Maria Bonita—a reference to the girlfriend of Lampião, the famous outlaw and folk hero of the Northeast, and also to the young girl's striking beauty and innate intelligence.

"We're gonna wait for him," declared the younger, sinking Maria's hopes. "You gonna offer us something for supper?"

There was nothing but a smidgen of manioc. Nobody had gone fishing in recent days and their stocks were running low.

"The boss—Benjamin—and Adriano are bringing something," she replied. "All we've got right now is manioc."

"It's getting dark. We're gonna stay here the night," was the reply. "Aren't you gonna at least offer us one of them chickens?"

"The chickens belong to the boss. I can't touch them," Maria explained. "Manioc is all we're going to eat too."

"Looks like that boss of yours is in no hurry to get home. We're gonna hang our hammocks on the porch here," said the younger man, and Maria was scared stiff by the way he looked at her.

She knew that kind of look. It felt like he was checking her over as if she were for sale. Her stepfather had been looking at her the same way just before Adriano came into her life. She was trembling inside but tried not to show it. She took the children into the house and, as if forgetting about the windows, locked the door in the vague hope it might provide a touch of safety. She knew the wood was rotten and one meager kick would break the door open.

It was so hard to believe. She'd faced the worst day of her life and now this. She remembered that Adriano's two shotguns were in the other house. Everything had happened so quickly; she'd moved into the main house and forgotten about the weapons. She still had the small machete but it was not enough to take on those men.

In the darkness of night, she lay alongside the three children, praying as she listened to the mutt's frantic barking. Her head was spinning. Perhaps they could flee in the dark. It sounded like the intruders were drinking outside and their voices got louder and louder. Suddenly a shot rang out and she heard a long shuddering howl from Tata as the men guffawed. A little while later, they rattled the door knob. When they saw it was locked, they threw themselves against it.

"Lady, open the door!"

"Think about the kids!" said the other one.

"Leave us alone! The children are sleeping," Maria begged.

"They can keep on sleeping as far as we care." Maria recognized the older man's voice. The next second the door gave way under their weight and they almost fell inside, bringing with them the heavy smell of *cachaça* and a glint of moonlight.

Wielding her small machete, Maria positioned herself in front of the children, who were whimpering now. Isaías tried to move in front of her, but she pushed him back so fiercely that he obeyed.

"Don't hurt us!" the boy cried out. "God will punish you."

"We wanna have a talk with you, lady. If you act right and the little ones shut up, nothing bad's gonna happen," said the younger man, who seemed more sober. The older one could barely stand up.

Maria knew full well what they wanted to talk about. If she had a real weapon, she'd have a chance. Again, she bitterly regretted her oversight. But in any case, it would be a dangerous long shot. She needed to protect the children at all costs. She owed that to Adriano, Benjamin, and Nina.

She felt a strange calm come over her, and her body seemed to fall asleep. She dropped her weapon and said to the children, "You stay here! Isaías, watch the girls and don't let anyone leave. I'll be right back."

She walked over to the door and pushed the two men out of her way.

"Not here," she said. She left the house and headed over to the storage shed where the rubber was. The men followed in silence.

The younger one came at her first, ripping off her clothes and throwing her to the ground, while the older fellow held the door open so there'd be some light and he could watch the show. Deadened all over, Maria sensed only the strong smell of sweat and booze and a thick, shaky hand running over her body. She put up no resistance whatsoever because she wanted it over in a hurry. She shut out the pain, and tried not to acknowledge it when the man pushed inside her. He tried to kiss her but she turned her face away. No, not that, that would be even more revolting. Maria got lucky—he was so eager he didn't last long. She felt a perverse sense of victory. What a pathetic excuse of a man.

Then came the old fellow, drooling all over. He tried to suck at her breasts and managed to hurt her with the few teeth he had. She ignored the physical pain and tried to ignore the stench and quell her revulsion. He was so drunk he didn't really take her and was soon satisfied. Though the whole nightmare lasted but a few minutes, in Maria's mind it felt like endless torture, a slow, deep suffering, a rage that wouldn't go away.

"Before we leave tomorrow, there'll be more," the younger one informed her. He helped his buddy get up and leave the shed.

Maria heard the words like a prison sentence. She threw on some clothes and rushed to the stream not far away. There she washed off as much of her tormenters' saliva and semen as she could. She was done in and sick to her stomach. She'd never experienced anything so repugnant. No, tomorrow there'd be no more.

After she'd made sure the two men were snoring in their hammocks, she furtively entered the house, where she found Isaías and the girls huddled in a corner.

"Quiet!" she whispered. "We're going to get out of here while they're asleep. We can't make a sound. Isaías, you go out first with Alice and then I'll come right out with Lídia. We'll meet behind that big ceiba tree."

It was remarkable: 5-year-old Alice and 4-year-old Lídia obeyed without a tear. Maria took the time to change out of her clothes, reeking of sweat and tobacco, and into some of Nina's clean things. She felt a little better right away, as if she'd finally taken a complete bath.

The thought flitted momentarily through her head that she could slice the younger fellow's throat with the machete as he snored carefree in his hammock. The old guy was still drunk, so getting the best of him would be no great challenge. That way she could save the *pelas*, which were her only possession. But thinking of the children, she discarded the idea. It would be too risky. When they were walking down the dark path Maria knew so well, tiny Lídia in her arms, she saw a shadow. It was Benjamin's donkey, who must have run away in fright when it heard the gunshot. Then she felt something rub up against her legs. It was Tata's tail.

"Great! You got away too! Now don't go barking." Tata and the donkey came along in silence, as if they'd gotten the message.

The first thing was to clean the two shotguns and get them ready. Thank God there was enough ammunition. In the darkness of night, she took the donkey and tied it up in the middle of the forest, far from any trail. If her plan worked, he'd have the crucial job of carrying the latex to Fortaleza do Abunã. She couldn't lose him now. She took the two girls to another hiding spot and asked them to keep quiet. She went back to the house and gave Isaías one of the shotguns. She told him that as soon as he heard a shot, he should say the Lord's Prayer, point the gun straight up, and pull the trigger. Then he had to say another Lord's Prayer, load the gun, and shoot again. Then he should run over to where the girls were hiding and wait for her.

"And if something happens and you take too long?" he asked. Maria could tell he was petrified.

It was asking a lot of a mere 6-year-old, even if he was a denizen of the forest. Luckily, Adriano had already started teaching him to hunt and handle a gun.

"Nothing's going to happen. I'll be right back!" she reassured him, and Isaías could tell his mother had made up her mind. He asked no more questions.

With the other shotgun in her hand, Maria headed back towards the main house, looking for the intruders' cart. It was dark and all indications were that both men were still sleeping. The cart was standing by the side of the house but their donkey was tied up a little farther ahead, near a waterhole.

Maria waited patiently until daybreak. Then she went over to the animal, which gave a nervous snort. She patted his head gently, took the gun, and shot him right where she'd petted him. The donkey collapsed and she ran full speed to take hiding in a protected spot behind the trees, where she still had a good view. It wasn't long before the younger fellow dashed out in that direction, gun in hand. At that moment another shot rang out, farther away, and the man stopped short in fright. Then he hurried even faster towards the cart. Maria thought about nothing but the lessons she'd learned from Adriano. She aimed as carefully as she'd been taught and with a firm hand squeezed the trigger. She heard the gun's explosion, felt it kick against her shoulder, and watched the man drop to the ground. She knew she'd hit him but couldn't be sure he wasn't simply wounded. She remained frozen in place, waiting to see if he moved. Then she saw the older man running towards the cart and she got ready to fire again. Another shot rang out from the distance—Isaías was doing as he'd been told. The panicked old man stopped near the spot where his partner had been hit and Maria watched as he hid behind a tree in an attempt to save himself from the invisible enemy. He shouted out his buddy's name a few times but got no response. Then he spotted something that left him even more panicky. Maria didn't know exactly what it was. He'd probably spotted the bodies of the donkey and his partner. In total despair, he leapt out of his place of protection and sprinted towards a trail that some miles farther along would lead him out of the rubber forest. He was still within close range. Maria calmly raised her weapon, thought once again of Adriano and his lessons, and pulled the trigger. Precisely as she'd intended, the bullet just grazed him. It was only meant to scare him. To be on the safe side, she stayed in her hiding spot a bit longer, but when she was sure there was no more movement in the area, she strode quickly over to where the children were hiding. She didn't want to so much as glance at the body of the man she'd just killed.

Their road to Fortaleza do Abunã was open now. She could hook Benjamin's donkey up to the intruders' cart. It would fit at least seven *pelas*, plus Lídia and Alice. She, Isaías, and Tata could walk. The village wasn't that far. In two or three days at most, if all went well, they'd be there. The nine heavy balls of rubber that couldn't be taken on the first trip had to be hidden without a trace, and then all Maria would need would be a little rest, some chicken soup, and a good night's sleep.

She was physically and emotionally spent. On the two most agonizing days of her life, she had buried the man she loved, along with her other loved ones; she'd been raped; and then she'd killed a man. As if this weren't enough, she'd spent the day loading and hiding latex, while Isaías hunted down the few remaining chickens and tied them up. In exhaustion, she slaughtered and feathered one of the birds to make the soup that she and the three children needed. After their meal, they laid down in silence beneath their only mosquito netting to sleep one last night in the house that had been the couple's home for six years. The children were so weary they soon fell asleep. Maria, her arms around them, did not shed a single tear. Instead, she lay awake, remembering the happy times that were now part of a distant past.

In the early hours of the morning before they left, as if living out a nightmare that didn't want to end, she took the children to bid farewell to their loved ones.

"Goodbye, Quatro Ases! Goodbye Nina, Benjamin, and angel Ariel! Goodbye Adriano, my love!"

CHAPTER 3
THE GARIMPO

The rain finally stopped and visibility was much better. Still, heavy clouds hung menacingly, presaging a big storm. It was only a matter of time before another downpour struck.

"Let's speed things up a bit so we can get there in time to do some work and still get back in the late afternoon."

It was a few short miles from the city of Porto Velho to the gold-mining operations, an area known as the *garimpo*, but the road was barely passable in the rain.

"The repair shop we're going to visit is just a little ways beyond Teotônio waterfalls. Now that the visibility's better, get ready to see something you can't even begin to imagine. Hundreds of floats and dredges jockeying for a place on the crowded Madeira River.

"Isn't it dangerous to show up like this, completely unarmed? Even more so because we've got a huge supply of outboard motors, the most coveted piece of equipment around here."

The two men were squeezed into a pickup truck loaded with assorted boxes, some on the luggage rack and others inside the cab. The road was utterly deserted and a muddy, potholed mess. Some holes were craters so deep you had to keep a keen eye out for any tracks that might have been left by vehicles that had managed to get through, and pray it would all be fine.

"The worst danger, Gabriel my friend, is not when you go in, but when you come out of the *garimpo*. That's when everyone's carrying gold, the currency around here. Every once in a while, someone will get ambushed while they're heading to Porto Velho to sell their yield from several days' work. The folks on the rigs always have a good idea how much everyone is producing. There's always somebody willing to supply the gangs of thieves that hang around here with valuable information for a small price."

"And aren't we in some danger? We'll be just as unarmed on our way out as we are now."

Oleg answered in Portuguese that was fluent but marked by a slight, hard-to-place accent: "That's why we don't carry money or checks, much less gold. And everyone knows that. Our orders are all paid in advance by direct deposit to Berimex. I've sold and delivered over a thousand outboard motors and never had any trouble—but I'm still sure we run something of a risk. As you'll see, the top-selling outboard around here is our brand, a 40 horsepower. It's what everyone uses on their motorboats to get around fast. Anything smaller is no match for the current on the Madeira River."

"I still don't understand why we've got such a strong position in this market. Sure, our motors are excellent, but our competitors offer similar products. How do you explain the fact that we control such a large slice of the business?"

"Really, our biggest advantage is that we offer immediate delivery of so many different replacement parts. It's our job to guarantee a smooth and steady flow of parts—and that's the secret to our success. We make a lot more selling spare parts than we do on the motors themselves. A bunch of equipment breaks down every day, leaving the guys high and dry. Without the parts we supply, life in the *garimpo* would be a lot tougher. Look, we're almost there. You can see the river."

The pickup stopped at a makeshift barricade, where a few armed men asked questions about their cargo and destination. But they didn't ask for a single document. In the distance, Oleg and Gabriel could see floating structures of all sizes jammed together, some two-stories tall, some much smaller. A number were brand new and gleaming from care; many were falling apart. They were packed in so tight it was hard to make out the muddy waters of the Madeira River.

"We're looking for Mr. Vicente Amorim, the fellow who owns the repair shop," Oleg said. He pointed to a large rig anchored by the riverbank, right near the barricade.

Everybody in the *garimpo* knew Amorim. He'd set up shop in those parts ages before anyone else, and his rig was strategically moored to dry land, right next to the entrance to the area. When you arrived at the site, you couldn't help but see Amorim's huge rig plastered with crude drawings of trademarks, representative of a vast array of manufacturers of outboard motors and parts.

Oleg parked his pickup in the shade of a large tree and honked his horn. Two men quickly came out and climbed up the riverbank to begin unloading the cargo. It was the same routine week after week, and everyone knew his job.

"Two motors and all the spare parts belong to you fellows, but the other four are for other buyers, who'll be picking them up today. Where's Amorim?"

"He's been down with Marlene for a week, taking it easy," the men told him. Gabriel and Oleg went into the repair shop.

More than twenty motors were piled in there, some partially disassembled, others nothing but the housing. Lying in a hammock by the river's edge was a man of sixty or more. He struggled a bit to get out and went over to the visitors. Like practically everyone in the mining business there, he was wearing nothing but baggy shorts, accentuating his small, skinny body. From a distance, he might be taken for a boy of no more than 15. He held a book in his hand. Gabriel was surprised when he saw it was *One Hundred Years of Solitude*, by his well-known namesake and Colombian Nobel laureate, Gabriel García Márquez.

"This is the famous Vicente Amorim, owner of the biggest and best repair shop in these parts and proprietor of the only library, whose holdings he kindly puts at the disposal of everybody in the business. He's a very respected fellow, considered a real authority. What's more, he's the most voracious reader and best joke teller I know.

"Mr. Amorim, this is my friend Gabriel. He's here from Manaus to help me sell outboard motors and parts. I expect to spend more time at the car and truck dealership in Porto Velho from here on in. Gabriel has a reputation as a top-rate mechanic. He trained at the Berimex garage. If you've got anything that's giving you real trouble, he can help you out better than me."

Amorim was pleased with the news. There was no shortage of finicky motors, and the mechanics who helped him were nothing but amateur odd-jobbers. Amorim asked Oleg if the order was complete; receiving an affirmative reply, he told his men to inventory it. When Gabriel saw that neither his boss nor Amorim was going to supervise the inventory himself, he realized how much the two men trusted and respected each other.

Amorim invited them to sit down.

"I brought the two outboards that Alemão purchased last week, another one for Ceará, and another for Ivanildo Nóvoa. They'll be picking them up this afternoon," Oleg said.

"Great. I've got another parts order. And I sold another 40-hp motor to a fellow that just got here from way down south, in Rio Grande do Sul."

Gold seekers from all over Brazil and even abroad were flooding into the Madeira River mining region in search of fast and easy money in what was reputed to be a new El Dorado. A lot of them were poor and had little to their names, but among them were some adventurers flush with cash and material assets. A number of highly educated people were also borne along by this huge wave—it wasn't hard to find geologists, engineers, and doctors who couldn't resist the lure of filthy lucre. There was even one psychiatrist. While the majority were Brazilians from all corners of the country, a wide range of foreigners came as well, with Bolivians, Chileans, Peruvians, and even Americans and Koreans completing the colorful palette of fortune hunters. It was the 1980s—the heyday of the business—and around one thousand barges and dredges lined the Madeira, their hunger insatiable.

"You really should have lunch at Lola's, Amorim suggested. "It's been completely remodeled. The food is great and they serve delicious fish. Not to mention, Dona Sandra wants to talk to you, Russo."

That's when Gabriel learned that Oleg's nickname on the river was Russo—"Russian."

"What do you mean? I've eaten there a bunch of times, and I've seen her there, but I don't know her personally."

"I told her about you and she wants to meet you. You can go over there now. She's on the houseboat." Amorim was insistent.

"In that case, I'd like to leave our lunch boxes for Dona Marlene," Gabriel announced, smiling proudly because he'd remembered Amorim's wife's name.

"Marlene?" The men glanced at each other and snickered.

"'Marlene' is our nickname for malaria around here. It isn't hard to tell *you're* new to the mining business, a real greenhorn—a *brabo* as we call them! People who don't know our jargon are lost. The story goes that there was this prospector who calls up his wife to tell her he's been in bed with Marlene, and she shoots back at him, 'Big deal, I'm shacked up with the neighbor'." Amorim chuckled at his own joke.

"My crew's going to check the parts first, and that takes a while. In the meantime, my helmsman Moicano can take you on the *voadeira* to visit the *fofoca*," Amorim suggested, still laughing.

Oleg translated the jargon for Gabriel: "A *voadeira*'s a motorboat that's used to tug dredges or just to get around. A *fofoca* is the whole bunch of floats and dredges at a prospecting site—in fact, it means the whole site and everything that happens there. There must be about 400 dredges and other rigs at this *fofoca* alone."

"So leave the lunch for my hired hands, and let's get going," said Amorim. Ferried by Moicano in a flat-nosed motorboat, they zigzagged back and forth between rigs, getting to see a bit of the area. Gabriel soon concluded that the men inhabiting this strange and solitary world all had an urgent, compulsive need to tell stories, whose veracity could never be tested. The name *fofoca*, thought Gabriel, was very well deserved—in Portuguese it literally means "gossip." They made quick and frequent stops at a wide variety of rigs, and in between Oleg explained, "This is the low season. It's still raining a lot, and the waters are very high and the current strong. The churning river carries these enormous trunks—veritable icebergs—at a remarkable speed. They can do some serious damage if not spotted in time. Many floats—big ones, small ones—have been destroyed and a lot of people swallowed up by the water. Only boom dredges, because they're so big, can risk operating when the river's at its crest, but it's not easy for them either. Almost everyone stops work and takes the opportunity to go off on vacation or visit their family or do maintenance work on their equipment. But in less than a month, the rains stop and the water level slowly drops again. And the *fofoca* is back to normal, bustling with all sorts of activities and running around the clock. Only half a dozen rigs and floating platforms will stay at this base: Amorim's, the floats that sell supplies, and Sandra's. All the rest will spread out along the river, fighting for any remaining space."

"I've noticed different types of equipment right alongside each other, some with huge towers. Looks like there's more than one way to mine," Gabriel said.

"Yeah, you'll see both floats and dredges. I'll explain the difference later. Let's stop at Alemão's rig first. He's going to pick up his motors this afternoon. He's a longstanding Berimex customer—knows Licco and my cousin Daniel Hazan, but he still hasn't managed to get us to sell on credit. There's no selling on credit in this business. It's too risky. Even worse with the runaway inflation that's been plaguing the country in recent years. Credit's a thing of the past in Brazil."

Moicano steered the motorboat up to a large, well-tended two-story dredge that looked more like a huge houseboat. They were received by a hired hand who looked wary at first but relaxed as soon as he recognized Moicano. He started jabbering away and, like a typical prospector, the talk soon went into the favorite local topic: some place along the river, the *fofoca* was enjoying a boom; abundant amounts of gold were being brought up and everybody was filling his pockets.

"Around here, near Teotônio Falls on the Upper Madeira, the gold's thinning out; the river's given all it can. Alemão isn't here anymore. He headed over to Palmeiral, where we're setting up a bigger, fancier dredge. They're hauling up a lot of gold there now—it's a real boom. The new motors you brought us are for there."

Oleg asked if he could show Gabriel around the dredge. The hired hand gave his okay though he seemed somewhat reluctant. "Alemão doesn't like having people he doesn't know on the dredge, but since we're not working right now, and you're our suppliers, I'll let you take a look. This is a top-of-the-line suction dredge. We don't use divers, and you'll notice it has hydraulic controls. It's got a powerful 10-inch suction pump that hooks up to a truck engine. The iron boom digs up the riverbed and the sediment and gravel gets sucked up through that pipe and deposited in that big sluice box. We can go down almost 100 feet and take out up to 13 cubic yards. Our new dredge is going to have a boom that can reach down 160 feet. Its engine will be even more powerful, with a 12-inch pump. There's going to be no stopping us!" the prospector boasted.

"These are classy cabins," Gabriel observed in surprise. The second story had four rooms, plus the kitchen and bathroom.

"The big room is Alemão's. When he's here, that makes four *mansos*—experienced prospectors—plus the cook," the hired hand explained.

"The workers and the cook each get 5% of the yield. The cook washes clothes and does the cleaning too. The manager gets twice that and the rest goes to the owner, who pays for maintenance and other expenses."

Gabriel also learned that *mansos*, unlike the inexperienced *brabos*, were familiar with the whole production cycle and all the machinery.

"A good crew is vital," Oleg pointed out. "The rain is starting up again. Let's have lunch at Lola's. You can see the girls' famous floating establishment and meet the owner, Dona Sandra."

The restaurant was nearby. It was a spacious wooden structure, clean and well maintained. But it was the building next door that caught Gabriel's eye, a two-story wooden structure that looked liked a floating hotel.

"You can meet some of the girls today. At night the restaurant turns into a real swinging dance joint. The hotel is next door—or the brothel, to put it bluntly. Best to keep your distance. Even though Sandra makes sure the girls have periodic check-ups, there's lots of disease around here."

Moicano had just docked the motorboat when a tall, husky fellow with a gun appeared and gave the three passengers a careful once-over. When he saw one of them was Oleg, he broke into a grin. "Look who showed up!" he practically shouted. "Russo's back! Leave your guns with me and come on in."

"Hey there, pal! By now you should know we don't carry guns."

Shaking his head in a clear show of disapproval over such foolhardy bravura, the guard stood by to let them in.

A strange-looking older woman came over to them, clad in elegant attire that clashed with their surroundings. She had fire-red hair and big blue eyes and was sitting in a wheelchair, pushed by a blond woman of athletic build.

"You must be Oleg Hazan, better known as Russo. What a pleasure to meet you. Did you come to dine at my humble restaurant?"

"The pleasure's all mine. Yes, I did, and I've brought my colleague, Gabriel. Mr. Amorim said you'd like to speak with me."

"Yes, I would. You look an awful lot like your Uncle Licco. You've got his face, his sing-song voice, even his accent! Come in, please—you're my guests. We're serving a delicious grilled flagtail today."

Despite the fact that she was a madam running a business in the heart of the Amazon—one of the most dangerous, violent spots in the world—Dona Sandra was well educated and soft spoken. She owned the restaurant-cum-nightclub, whorehouse, and hotel, and ran them all with an iron fist. She brooked no unruliness from her "protégées"—as she called the prostitutes—or from her clients, who had to be unarmed and properly dressed. She was a business woman who took all her affairs seriously, especially the quality of services rendered.

While Oleg enjoyed his lunch—the food was tasty and the portions generous—he kept asking himself how she knew Uncle Licco. The story eventually came up.

"Back in my days in Manaus, thirty years ago, I met your aunt and uncle. We played tennis together twice a week and stayed at the same *banhos*. Licco and Berta were two of the finest people I've ever known. My husband worked at the refinery for a time, when Licco and Berta were Mr. Isaac Sabba's right hands. Then everything fell apart. My husband died young, and here I am, old and crippled. I heard Berta passed away not long ago. How's Licco doing?"

"Uncle Licco's in good health but he hasn't really gotten his spirit back. My aunt was always his pillar, his safe harbor, and he was always strong and happy when she was around. Now the floor's gone out from under him," Oleg replied.

Gabriel couldn't figure out why his attention kept wandering to the blond girl pushing the wheelchair. She was extraordinarily attentive to the old lady. She didn't say a word the whole while, just standing there behind Sandra, at her total beck and call.

"We could go on talking like this forever, but that's not why I called you here. Amorim told me you're thinking about building a new dredge. Well, I've got a nearly new suction dredge that's in mint condition—someone gave it to me to pay off a debt. It's anchored upstream at a prospecting site called Palmeiral. There's a lot more going on there now, and that's where my daughter Mariana and I will be moving when our new business is ready. We're building a new restaurant and hotel there. If you're interested, the dredge is yours. It'd be a pleasure doing business with Licco's nephew."

"That explains it," Gabriel thought. "The blond is her daughter." But he couldn't believe his ears: his boss, cousin to Daniel Hazan, president of Berimex, wanted to go into prospecting.

Oleg said nothing for a moment. Then he replied, "Well, given that my friend Amorim has spilled the beans, no point hiding it. I have been giving the idea some thought, but I haven't got enough money to buy a good dredge and then still have something left to cover start-up costs. Anyway, I'd need a few days to think it over. I've been wanting to open my own business for a while now. I'm planning on stopping by Amorim's office next week and I could take a look at the rig then. Can you wait a few days?"

"The dredge is yours. I'll tell them to anchor it up next to Amorim's repair shop. In your case, I'd be willing to make you a good price and even let you have it on credit. I can easily wait two weeks, until the start of next season. Something I'm curious about, Oleg. What nationality are you? Your aunt and uncle are Hungarian if I'm not mistaken, but Amorim always calls you Russo."

Oleg had to smile. "It's a long story. My aunt and uncle are Bulgarian, not Hungarian. My mother's Russian—like my nickname says—but I was born and brought up in Bulgaria and think of myself as Bulgarian, like them. I escaped the 'communist paradise' and hold Israeli citizenship now. I was in the Army there and that's where I went to college. So I'm a Bulgarian Jew and an Israeli citizen who is thinking about becoming a naturalized Brazilian. Pretty straightforward, isn't it?"

"You've certainly been around for someone your age."

Oleg chuckled and got up to say goodbye.

"Thank you for lunch. The food was excellent. We've got to see to Amorim's order now and still get back to Porto Velho today, before we get any more rain. I'd like to hit the road before dark. I'll be back here in two weeks."

"When you do come back, you can stay at my hotel. It's also the best nightclub on the Madeira River. Tell your uncle that you met Sandra Reis, wife of Ricardo Reis, from the refinery in Manaus. He might remember me. If we close this deal, I'm going to throw in a bonus: an Israeli Uzi. I'm sure you're familiar with it. We call the prospectors who go around here unarmed 'ducks', because they're sitting ducks for all the bad guys in the place. Losing a handsome Greek god like yourself, a real Hollywood heartthrob, just out of sheer reckless-ness—that would be a tremendous waste. You can't walk around here unarmed."

That's when Gabriel realized that what had really caught his attention about the blond wasn't anything about her looks but the natural way she had one of those automatics leaning up against the wheelchair.

When they left, Moicano took a short-cut back to Amorim's that got them there in no time at all. Oleg was deep in thought and a tad edgy, so Gabriel figured it best not to bother him with any questions. Amorim confirmed receipt of the parts and then asked about their visit.

"What did you think of Sandra? Did she tell you about her dredge? I know it well. Depending on the price, it could be a real steal."

"I guess Sandra—owner of Lola's brothel—knew my aunt and uncle thirty years back. How'd she end up in the *garimpo*?"

"Of course she knew them. It's quite a story. She was a real looker and married well. Her husband died young and she inherited a lot in money and jewels. She was lonely, and needy, and she had the bad luck of falling for a con artist who took total advantage of her. He got his hands on the bulk of her money and when that ran out, he beat her—more than once. He was after the jewels he knew she'd hidden. They were living in Porto Velho then. One of the beatings was so vicious that she lost consciousness and fell and hurt herself so bad that she could never walk again. The bastard beat Mariana too—she was just a baby—and then he took off. Nobody heard anything from or about him for ages. Years later he was found dead; he'd been brutally murdered in a hotel room in Cuiabá. Rumor has it that Sandra—it was a miracle she'd survived his last attack, and by then she owned Casa da Lola nightclub—well, that she'd taken out a contract on him, but nobody ever proved anything. Even if that's true, I like the woman and have a great deal of respect for her. We play cards twice a week and we're good friends. She's had a hard life, paraplegic and all, but even if she is the madam of a brothel, she's a good, decent, generous person. She's got a lot of power here in the *garimpo*, but elsewhere she bears the brunt of all the biases that society has against people like her. Her daughter—the blond who's always pushing her wheelchair—is her sole relative in the world. They love and really look out for each other. In fact, Mariana is a veritable guard dog," Amorim said. "And she's quite a shot! You need to see her. My son, Renato, has had his eye on her for years but they've only started dating recently. They go out once in a while, always with the story that they're going to have some ice-cream. No clue why the subterfuge—they're adults. But besides, she'll never leave her mother."

Precisely as Oleg had planned, the pickup left Porto Velho before sundown. Their orders had all been delivered and now their only cargo was an outboard motor that couldn't be fixed at the makeshift repair shop on the platform. Nobody asked them a thing at the barricade, and on they drove. Just as night was falling and it seemed the day would come to an uneventful close, out of nowhere a pickup appeared behind them, its headlights on bright, and another barrier loomed before them.

Oleg barely had time to warn Gabriel in a low voice. "It's an ambush. Just stay calm and don't make any sudden movements."

From behind the barrier, armed men ordered them to get out with their hands up. It was clear the pickup behind them was part of the trap. Blinded by the high beams, Oleg and Gabriel could only make out the silhouette of a fat man getting out of the truck. "Your weapons!" he shouted.

"We're not armed. We sell motors. We're not prospectors. We don't get paid in money or gold and we're not carrying anything of any value. The only thing we've got is an old outboard—belongs to Vicente Amorim."

Oleg noticed that the name Amorim got a reaction. The men searched the cab but found no guns or gold.

Less threatening now, the fat man let them put down their arms and asked how much money they had.

"Not much. Two indigents," the fat man muttered after counting the money. Then he ordered his men to siphon off most of their fuel. "Leave just enough for the suckers to reach the road."

Stripped of their meager cash, very little diesel in their tank, but with their motor untouched and breathing a sigh of relief, Oleg and Gabriel were allowed to go on their way. As soon as they'd made it around the first bend without taking a bullet from behind, Gabriel said, "My God! I don't know if I want to take this job. Better we crapped our pants than took a bullet, but still... Your mention of Amorim saved our lives."

"No question that Amorim helped us—they didn't even touch his motor. Now I see why Dona Lola wanted to give me a semi-automatic. These folks don't fool around—they've got a real war arsenal."

The lights of the city soon appeared, along with the first gas station.

"Let's fill her up," Oleg said.

"With what money?"

Oleg smiled, got out, and felt under the chassis. He pulled out a little plastic bag with a few bills inside.

"Better safe than sorry. Now we'll have enough fuel to get home."

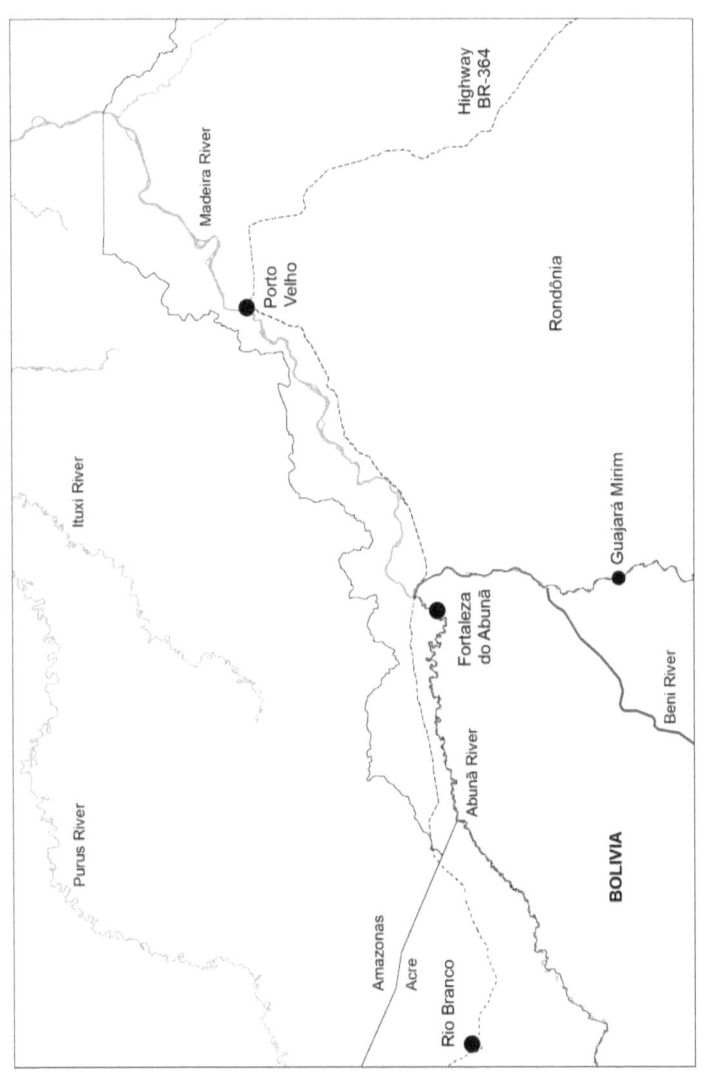

CHAPTER 4
THE PROSPECTOR

"Uncle Licco, of course things are going just fine at Berimex. I mean it! It's not about wanting a raise. It's just that the *garimpo* is the best place for me to carve out my own space for myself, without needing anybody else's help, and make some good money besides. I'm thinking about buying this dredge, and you're the first to know. I haven't even talked to my father or to Daniel or Sara yet."

As so often the case back in the 1980s in the Amazon, the phone connection wasn't very good and Oleg had trouble understanding his uncle's arguments on the other end of the line. Still, to judge from Licco's tone of voice, Oleg could tell he was wholeheartedly against the idea—furious in fact. Then they were cut off, much to Oleg's relief. Next to his father, David, Licco was the most important person in Oleg's life and it was clear the conversation with him would be tougher than he'd imagined.

The phone rang and this time it was Daniel. "Oleg, what's this about your wanting to be a prospector? Dad's devastated, and he's probably already on the phone to Uncle David."

"Daniel, don't get me wrong. Everything's just fine at Berimex, and I'm grateful to you all. But I just need to prove to myself that I can make it on my own. It's a need that's stronger than I am."

Neither of them said anything for a moment. Then Oleg announced, "I'm going to need two outboard motors at a very good price."

"If you promise you won't say anything to dad, I'll give you the two motors—very grudgingly. I'm worried about your safety. The stories you hear! You know very well the *garimpo* is far from a promised land. My father's never going to accept your decision—especially because he thinks he's responsible, since he was the one who sent you out to the *garimpo* in the first place. Get ready for a lot of pressure from him and Uncle David. I've got to go now. Let's talk again later today." Daniel sounded weary.

Oleg tried to get back into his work but the phone rang yet again. Now it was Sara, Daniel's sister.

"Cousin, I just heard you've decided to leave Berimex and I want you to know I'm behind you one hundred percent. Now, the idea of your becoming a prospector—that makes my hair stand on end. Rein it in a little, will you?! There's a lot of other things you can do."

Oleg thought about what an incredible woman Sara was, like her mother Aunt Berta before her. "Licco and Daniel want the best for me too," he told himself, "but, no surprise, everybody—without a single exception—is against my idea of going to the *garimpo*."

"Cous', I promise to behave myself and be very careful. I'm going to go after some real nice nuggets just for you." That's all he could think of to say.

Sara laughed. "You're no kid, and I hope you know what you're doing. It's high time you got married and had some kids, and the *garimpo* is not exactly the place for you to find a wife. Think it over. And for your information, the gold along the Madeira River is all powder—so you can save your nuggets for your future wife!"

She was trying to keep it light, but Oleg could sense how worried she was.

He had just gotten off the phone with Sara when it rang again. This time it was his father, David, calling from Israel. Oleg got a knot in his throat but he tried to tell the story he'd repeated so often that morning, calmly and patiently. His father's reaction was unexpected.

"Oli, my son, I have total confidence in you and all I ask is that, whatever you do, do it in moderation and keep your wits about you. We've been through a lot together and I'm sorry I can't be with you this time around. I'm getting too old for this kind of adventure and all I know is I need some grandchildren now. You're the only one who can take care of that problem for me! Licco's got a bunch already. He's really worried about you, and I imagine he's on his way to the airport in Manaus so he can visit you. He knows the trade and the region like nobody else, and you've got a duty to listen to him. Still, the decision is yours and I'll support it, whatever it is. Licco has always felt responsible for us and sometimes he forgets I'm already in my sixties and you're the same age as Sara. If you stick to your guns, he'll eventually give in. Between you and me, even though I can't join you for real, some day I'm going to visit the *garimpo* on the Madeira River. Just wait and see!"

Oleg felt better now that things had gone smoother with his father. It was good to feel his father's love—he'd always be his "little Oli." Whenever his father called him by that name, he knew what followed would be important. Though his dad was worried, he'd managed to lend his support.

Now he had to wear down his uncle's resistance. He called around to a few shops that made equipment and floating platforms for dredges. Some hours later, he did the math: he'd need 320 Troy ounces of gold to put together a good suction dredge. That was a lot of money and he only had half. He'd need another 16 ounces on top of that to get the dredge into the water and up and running. It would be a challenge, but it was nothing that could defeat a determined young man bitten by the bug of adventure and seduced by the glitter of gold.

ΦΦΦ

"I'm going to stay here until you come to your senses. Right now, I need to find a hotel and take a nice hot shower. We'll have dinner later and get it all out on the table."

"I've already booked you a room at Vila Rica hotel for a week," Oleg retorted.

"You knew I was coming?" Licco was taken aback. His nephew had a strange way of making him feel he didn't have a leg to stand on—just like his brother David. "Can I ask why a week? Is that how long this madness is going to last?"

"No, Uncle Licco. I knew you'd come because dad told me. I hope a week will be enough for me to convince you that I've made the right decision."

Licco held his tongue, and the two men got into the same pickup that had been ambushed on the muddy road two days earlier.

"Good thing this truck can't talk," Oleg thought. "If Uncle Licco knew what had happened over the last few days, he'd go ballistic."

Licco spent the next days trying as best he could to talk his nephew out of the idea of prospecting for gold. He considered Oleg a second son, one for whom he had fought desperately, by means both legal and illegal, helping him and his father make a breathtakingly audacious escape through the Iron Curtain. On the date of that event, nearly eleven years earlier, World War II had truly ended for the small Hazan family, at long last. Licco had still been savoring his re-united family's newfound tranquility, when life—as it so often happens—took a new twist and hit him hard yet again. Cancer took Berta, his partner since forever, and the wound simply didn't want to heal. And now, as if that hadn't been enough, Oleg, for no good reason at all, wanted to embark on a foolhardy, dangerous adventure. It was too much and Licco wasn't about to let it happen.

They ate dinner in silence. Only after they finished did Oleg tell his uncle about his latest trip to the *garimpo* and his visit with Sandra Reis.

"Of course I remember her and Ricardo. He worked a short while at the refinery and then set up office as a pharmaceutical agent. They were both good tennis players, and we'd meet them at the Bosque Club every week. Even though he was fanatic about playing sports, Ricardo had a massive heart attack and died young. We never heard from her after that. I remember she had long, black hair and blue eyes. She was very pretty— attractive and happy-go-lucky. She liked socializing and the couple attended every single party at all the most popular nightclubs back then—Acapulco, Ideal, Bosque, Rio Negro."

"The only pretty thing left are her eyes. Now her hair is dyed fire-engine red. She's old, paraplegic, and earns her living running a brothel. What's more, she's got a dredge she wants to sell me."

Licco wasn't about to back down. He was determined to keep his nephew from venturing into the forest.

"Forget it. You've been doing a great job here in Rondônia and our business is going strong in large part because of you. We can make the Porto Velho branch an independent company, and you could play a big role there. I'm certain that Daniel, Sara, and our partner

Gustavo will go along with the idea and would be more than happy to bring you in as a shareholder. I'll think it over a bit more, talk with everybody else, and make you a formal offer. That was a good dinner, and now I'm going to bed. We'll talk again tomorrow."

"Uncle Licco, thank you for everything, but I think it's important for you to know from the get-go that I won't accept your proposal, no matter how generous. I don't know yet if I'll be buying this dredge, or another one, but one thing I'm certain of: I'm going to spend some time in the *garimpo*."

From his nephew's tone of voice, he could tell Oleg was going to be as stubborn as his father, David.

Licco returned to his hotel, where he lay in bed in the solitude of his room and traveled back in time forty years to the forced labor camp in Somovit, Bulgaria, when his brother David had declared his plans to escape and join the armed resistance against the Bulgarian fascists and their German allies—over his brother's protests. After a tense conversation, the brothers had bid each other farewell in the midst of a heavy snowstorm, never to see each other for fifteen long years. At least under those circumstances, David had had good reason to follow a dangerous pathway, but that wasn't the case now.

ΦΦΦ

"Uncle Licco, Gabriel and I are going to Palmeiral tomorrow to deliver some motors and spare parts. I'm going to use the opportunity to take a look at Dona Sandra's dredge."

The week that Licco was supposed to spend in Porto Velho was already coming to an end and it was with chagrin and a sense of panic that he concluded Oleg wouldn't budge an inch. But Licco wasn't about to give up without a fight. "You and your damn dredge! Since it's such a big deal, I'm going too. You can't get rid of me that easy. Berimex sells so much to those folks that I guess there's no good reason why someone from top management hasn't ever set foot in a *garimpo*."

Worried about another ambush, Oleg tried to argue that federal highway BR-364—which started in the distant city of Limeira, down south in São Paulo state, and went through the states of Goiás, Mato Grosso, and Rondônia before ending in Rodrigues Alves, in Acre state—wasn't blacktopped. He pointed out that Palmeiral was nearly ninety miles away, the pickup would be packed…but it did no good.

"The truck doesn't have air-conditioning, but because of the dust, even though it's blazingly hot, we'll have to keep the windows closed for hours. We can't get there and back on the same day, not this time around, so we'll have to stay overnight in the *garimpo*. Since Casa da Lola Hotel isn't finished yet, we'll be sleeping in hammocks on Amorim's rig."

"I love a nice hammock! During our first year in Brazil, when we were still living in Belém, Berta and I slept in a hammock for ages. I'm going with you, and that's that!" Licco had an answer for everything and he had no intention of giving up easy.

"Alright, if that's the way you want it!" Oleg shot back. "We'll have to stock up on insect repellant because the place is infested with mosquitoes. We leave at six in the morning."

ΦΦΦ

The rains wouldn't let up and the road was worse than expected. Even with water blowing in, they had to keep the windows rolled halfway down so the air in the cab wouldn't go stale and the temperature would be somewhat tolerable. They passed some pickups and a number of taxis along the way, practically all of them junk heaps. The traffic was heavy in both directions, especially over the final stretch. Palmeiral was indeed a boom town.

It was noon by the time they arrived, exhausted and dripping wet. The delivery routine was the same, except for one detail: Gabriel and the manager both verified the order. Next to Amorim's rig was a dredge that looked deserted. They walked over to it and Oleg started explaining the workings of the huge collection of equipment.

"Uncle Licco, this here's a suction dredge. I imagine you've heard about the cruder rigs, the floats that are guided by divers. Modern dredges like this one are a lot different."

"Yes, I've heard of them—and I shudder when I remember the stories. Fellows suffocating to death because the diver couldn't see through the muddy water and got wound up in the hoses or, worse yet, because his buddies cut off his air when he signaled that the locale looked promising or had enough gold to be divided. I can't stand the thought of anyone doing that kind of a job, much less you! Do you have any idea how these vessels work, Oleg?"

"Uncle Licco, I've used my stint working at Berimex to learn a lot. I know that divers were really important on the old floats. It was up to them to pick out the best spot and position the hose to suck up the material and send it to the sluice box. They crew would cover the bottom of the box with big pieces of carpet and then separate the gold fragments from the carpet fibers. Fine particles of metal, heavier than the rest, got thrown back into the river." Oleg needed to show his uncle that he knew where he was stepping and that he'd made a wise decision. "All the hands on a float should be divers, and they have to keep switching out—nobody can stand to stay under for very long in that muddy water, and the process is only interrupted when they reach the target of their ambitions, the *despesca*—beating the carpets to remove the gold and then divvying up their 'catch'. Modern dredges like this one operate without divers. The controls are all hydraulic and the suction pump is hooked up to a boom, which can go down nearly a hundred feet. There's a big cutting drum on the end of the boom—sometimes called a pineapple, because that's what it looks like—it does the digging that used to be done by men. It stirs up the riverbed and sucks the material into the sluice box lined with carpet pieces."

"Well, I've got to admit you know all about the process. But I've heard mercury poisoning is a big problem. Not just the water but the air and every living creature around. It's vicious." Licco was not ready to admit defeat.

Gabriel had finished his work and came over to join them in time to hear Oleg's explanation. Oleg had done his prep work; he knew every single phase of the process, both the older processes that had really damaged the environment and the new ones too, ones that used methods less likely to cause mercury contamination. Licco tried to argue that the true extent of heavy metal contamination had yet to be measured and evaluated, but he decided to simply shut up.

In the *garimpo*, it's common practice to turn in early after a long hard day of work, especially when there's nothing happening in the gold-mining village or floating bars, both overflowing with prostitutes. Such was the case that day, and after dinner, rocking in the hammock, his eyelids drooping, Gabriel asked, "Oleg, do you know why they call Amorim's hired hand Moicano? Doesn't that mean Mohawk, like the hair cut?"

"It means 'Mohican', like the tribe. They're extinct now, but they wore their hair that way. There's that famous book, *The Last of the Mohicans*," Licco explained.

"Wasn't that by James Fennimore Cooper?" Oleg asked. "Amorim has that book in his library. I happen to know the story. But the fellow's name doesn't have anything to do with the Indian tribe or the haircut. His real name is Raimundo, but Amorim nicknamed him 'the last Mohican' and it stuck. And got shortened over time. The story goes like this: one fine day, Raimundo was coming back from his weekly break and he was all full of himself, boasting about how he'd finally talked this girl who worked as a cook on a big neighboring rig to go out with him. She'd turned him down every single time before and now he was strutting like a peacock. What he didn't know was that the girl quite often would relieve the sexual tensions of prospectors in exchange for a few modest grams of gold. Amorim was aware of her willingness to render such services, and since he never misses out on a chance to give somebody a good ribbing, he said, "You were the last man in the whole *fofoca* to screw the girl. The last Mohican!""

The three men couldn't stop laughing.

"Here I am, out in the middle of nowhere, beyond the back of beyond, in a completely strange place—and for the first time since Berta passed away, tonight I felt like laughing like in the old days. What would my friend Salvator have said if he'd come along with me on this crazy journey?" Snug in his hammock, the wheels in Licco's head wouldn't stop turning.

ΦΦΦ

More than forty years earlier, during World War II,
at the forced labor camp where Bulgarian Jews struggled to survive, Salvator had been Licco's closest
friend. Numerous sectors of the Bulgarian population
and of the country's Orthodox Church had fought the
idea of handing the Jews over to Hitler's Germany,
leading to a Solomonic solution: under this pressure,
and very reluctantly, the Bulgarian state, led by a pro-
German fascist government, ended up organizing its
own forced labor camps. While treatment in the camps
was cruel, they were not dedicated to the open extermi-
nation of the Jewish population and, in the final analy-
sis, were in fact responsible for saving most of their
prisoners, who otherwise would have been slaughtered
in Polish concentration camps. But Salvator was not a
healthy man and he had not withstood a harsh winter
under precarious living conditions; he passed away
shortly before the end of the war and liberation. The
friendship between the two men had been so strong that
ever since, whenever something unusual happened,
Licco called on his friend, who still seemed to occupy a
corner deep inside his soul. Salvator remained silent this
time, and Licco fell asleep, soothed by the rocking of
the hammock and the gentle breeze of a tropical night.

They hit the road early the next morning. Oleg joked to himself, "Not even the highway robbers and gunmen are up this time of day."

"Isn't this road dangerous?" Licco seemed to have read his nephew's mind.

"No, Uncle Licco, this season, when the water level is this high, there's not much production and the miners' satchels are empty. In fact, it's so slow that Lola's girls are resting and even the thieves have hit hard times!"

They took turns at the wheel and spent much of the ride in silence. When they were almost to Porto Velho, Oleg decided to speak up. "Uncle Licco, next week I've got a meeting with your friend, Dona Sandra, and I'm going to try to work out a deal on her dredge. All it needs are a few tests. The next step will be recruiting some experienced prospectors."

"Since I'm already here, I'll go with you. I still can't believe that that respectable woman now owns a brothel. I'd like to see her. Maybe our old friendship will help your negotiations." Licco had spoken without thinking, and he quickly tried to do some damage control. "Don't think I've suddenly decided to approve of your madness!"

Two days later, the pickup filled with spare parts and outboard motors parked under the tree next to Amorim's rig. The same workers unloaded the boxes again, and Oleg and Licco went to greet a frail Amorim, who came out to welcome them. The man had just recovered from his bout of malaria.

"Mr. Amorim, this is my uncle, Licco Hazan." Oleg promptly introduced the two men. "He wants to visit the *garimpo* and meet with Dona Sandra."

Amorim had already heard about Licco, from both Oleg and Sandra.

"In addition to being your client, I've heard a lot of good things about you," Amorim said, staring at Licco as if he'd known him a long while but couldn't quite place him. Then he broke into a broad grin. "You talk just like Russo—and look a lot like him. Sandra had mentioned that, but the resemblance is really striking."

"Well, my dear nephew Oleg is a new and improved version of me!"

"I'm joining you for lunch today. Sandra will be so happy to see you both. She hasn't stopped talking about Licco and his wife since Russo's last visit. She lives in the past! Tell me the truth, do you really know everything there is to know about regional Amazon products?"

"'Everything' is an exaggeration. But I did learn a lot with the men who saw potential in this land years ago and have been studying it ever since. True pioneers—four of them are very dear to me. I learned a lot from Isaac Sabba, Moysés Israel, Isaac Benzecry, and Samuel Benchimol. I've been exporting rosewood essential oil and copaiba balsam for thirty years. And yet I know a lot less than I'd like to. My late wife Berta and I bought a beautiful piece of land near Maués and I'm going to put in a rosewood plantation there."

Since Oleg was anxious to get negotiations with Sandra rolling, Amorim, Licco, and he climbed into the motorboat and Moicano took them straight to the restaurant. The bouncer recognized them right away and took them over to a small makeshift elevator, operated by two strong *caboclos* and a winch. They went up into the reserved area on the second floor, an airy room covered with a thatched roof.

"This is Sandra's private quarters. Very few people are ever allowed in here," Amorim explained in a low voice, almost whispering. "There's a nice master bedroom here. Next door is her daughter Mariana's room and a small office. Her wheelchair makes the trip fast in this elevator—and it's a security device too. Makes so much noise there's no way you can come up without being noticed. As you can see, it's also for security reasons that there's no stairs, and there's always one or two hired hands near the winch."

They had barely gotten settled in comfortable rocking chairs in the airiest part of the room when they heard women's voices, and then the elevator began making another trip. The wheelchair was rolled in backwards and even before Sandra could see the men who were waiting for her, she started talking. "So Russo made good on his word. I'm so glad Amorim came."

Mariana turned the wheelchair around and Sandra

102

could see the visitors. It took her a minute to react, as her memory processed the third person's face.

"My God, Licco!" She choked out the words as tears sprang to her blue eyes, eyes that lit up her face. "Mariana, take me to my room. I need to fix myself up!" Her voice was raspy, barely a mumble. "Give me a minute please. I'll be right back."

Something had hit Licco as well. Anyone paying close attention could sense he was seeing much more than some red-headed woman. Her blue eyes were still beautiful—the only thing unchanged in her face. Licco saw another woman peering out through them, slender, carefree, full of life—and standing next to his Berta, both women still young and beautiful. They were wearing white tennis skirts and held Dunlop rackets in their hands. It was a delicious memory but almost too painful. He wondered if he might not find a photograph like that among Berta's albums.

The length of Sandra's absence from the room signaled how she had spared no effort fixing herself up. She'd even added a pair of high-heel shoes to complete her elegance, which contrasted starkly with her bizarre surroundings, where men walked around half naked, wearing nothing but scanty trunks. The women usually wore simple but sexy shifts; they'd never think of wearing heels.

Some might have looked askance at this strange encounter, or even turned up their noses, but the feelings that neither Licco nor Sandra could hide prevailed above all else, recasting the strange and ugly as normal, moving, authentic.

"Sandra Reis, my dear friend!" Licco wanted to say something truly meaningful but couldn't find the words.

The emotions felt by the two old friends were palpable, and Oleg and Amorim kept a respectful silence.

"Sometimes the old life back in Manus seems like a far-off, surreal dream," was Sandra's reply.

Lunch was served. The conversation was somewhat awkward, going in starts and stops. Oleg was clearly eager to start negotiations over the dredge, but it was just as clear that Licco and Sandra were interested in other matters. Amorim didn't open his mouth either. Everyone could see it wasn't time to talk business. The past was speaking louder.

"Russo, how long will you all be staying here with us?" asked Amorim, interrupting a period of silence.

"We're going to spend the night at Dona Sandra's hotel."

"We're going to stay two nights," Licco announced to everyone's surprise. He was back to his old self. "I want some more time to talk with Sandra and get to know how things work in the *garimpo*. I've got a lot to learn. We'll have dinner together tonight and talk about the dredge. I want to visit Mr. Amorim's operation too. You'll be my guests for dinner."

ΦΦΦ

Casa da Lola—hotel-cum-brothel, as Oleg defined it—was a clean, sturdy two-story wooden houseboat that floated alongside the restaurant. Oleg and Licco stayed in the rooms farthest from the dining room, at the end of the hall, where the music would disturb them less. Apparently calm and peaceful during the day, the place turned into a noisy, crowded nightclub after dark. Sandra ordered the volume turned way down on the music those two nights, and the rooms abutting the visitors' stayed empty. She knew full well that the flimsy wooden walls of her establishment provided no sound-proofing whatsoever. It wouldn't have been the first time a guest was bothered by some raucous, ardent customer or by some girl putting on a shocking show as she reached (or faked) an orgasm. Sandra had a reputation for selecting women who actually loved their job, and she demanded commitment to the oldest profession, along with the creativity requisite to the trade.

In the *garimpo*, where there were over twenty men for every woman, the hookers provided an invaluable service. Sandra's protégées were examined once a month by a doctor brought in from Porto Velho. They also received lessons and advice from more experienced colleagues. There were rules (not always followed to a 't') that guaranteed the best and safest services at any brothel in the *garimpo*. The girls were taught to be dedicated to their jobs but also to take care of themselves and use condoms as often as possible.

Customer satisfaction was top priority, and the men were only free to go once they'd been demonstrably worn out, with nothing left to give. Just when a client thought he was through, the games had only just begun for Sandra's hot-blooded gals. Niara Nutbuster and Mocha Louca, the two in greatest demand, possessed indisputable skills, and their fame had spread through the *garimpos* at the speed of sound. Their customers were always delighted to confirm the veracity of the bawdy rumor about the two women: neither could bear to let a turgid phallus remain as such and would not cease their efforts until the organ was spent and limp. Both ladies took great pride in their noms-de-guerre. Some of their more zealous admirers—in a show of unforgiveable selfishness, the thorough absence of team spirit, and a lack of basic human solidarity towards the less financially privileged of the candidates waiting in line—were willing to pay any price for an entire night of unbridled pleasure. But few could actually stand up to it. Most collapsed within a few hours, unprepared for the physical rigors. Much to everyone's happiness, the ladies thus had time to see to every man's needs. Along with Dona Sandra's wise words about public health considerations and performance goals, she offered her pupils one specific piece of advice that they were never supposed to forget: "Everything goes in the *garimpo*—except losing your head over some scallywag. No self-respecting hooker falls in love!"

"I've told them to make a delicious oven-baked pirarucu—I had it set aside for special guests. We can have a nice quiet chat up here while the folks are enjoying themselves in the nightclub."

Sandra had changed again and even Mariana was dressed to the nines. The same couldn't be said of the men, who'd spent the afternoon visiting a number of floats, dredges, and even a small village that had sprung up around the mining activity. To wrap the day up, Moicano had taken them to one of the crystal-clear waterfalls near the *garimpo*, where the men went fishing and swimming when they managed to grab a few free hours. They were tired and starving.

Sandra seemed rejuvenated. She kept recalling yet another acquaintance from Manaus, and Licco—as relaxed and happy as Oleg had seen him in forever—recounted tales of friends from yesteryear, some still alive, others gone. The conversation flowed on and on, no end in sight.

"Sandra, you have to make a visit to Manaus. The peaceful little town you left behind is now a flourishing metropolis. You won't recognize it!"

"I've got my reasons for not going back to Manaus. I'll tell you sometime. Now let's get down to business: the dredge."

Oleg was happy Sandra had finally decided to talk business. She said, "A new suction dredge, on land, not yet assembled and put in the water, goes for about 320 Troy ounces worth of gold. It takes at least another 32

107

ounces to cover assembly, testing, and getting it into the water. My dredge was in use for a year and everything on it runs perfectly. It's even got pots and pans in the kitchen. You just need to stock it and off you go. The shape it's in now, I'd be willing to sell it to any buyer for 270 Troy ounces."

"I can witness to the fact that it works," Amorim said. "There've been other buyers who tried it out, but they didn't have enough of the green stuff."

"In Russo's case, I'd let it go for 255 ounces, and even accept installment payments. He could pay for part of it in the gold he produces."

"Oleg, my boy, we can't keep any secrets from Sandra. Tell me, how much money do you have right now?" When things were serious, Licco still used his nephew's given name.

"I've got exactly 160 Troy ounces, but I'm going to need at least 16 for start-up capital. I could pay 128 right now."

"Sandra, we'll pay you 225 ounces up front, and end of subject. I'm going to lend my nephew the equivalent of 95 ounces—since I don't have gold, I'll pay in *cruzeiros*. With inflation where it is, you'll have to turn around and invest it immediately." Licco was eager to close the deal.

"Good old Licco, a real businessman! The rig is yours, Russo, and you can start right away. My bank manager knows precisely what to do with my money. I'm moving to my new nightclub in a few days and I'll take care of your nephew as if he were the son I never had. Amorim's going to help me with that; he's moving to Palmeiral too. No way can he leave me without my card partner."

Oleg could hardly believe it. Well before he'd anticipated—and with the help of Licco, who'd been the biggest obstacle between him and the *garimpo*—he'd become the owner of a suction dredge.

"Uncle Licco, once again I owe you big time. Thank you!"

"Mazel Tov, Oleg—I mean, Russo. May God watch over you!"

When he saw his nephew grinning from ear to ear, Licco was happy despite the dread still lingering in his heart. He hugged him hard. "I hope I don't live to regret this," he said, feeling a tug at his soul. "Now off to bed with all of you. I'm still excited and wide awake. I'm going to enjoy a glass of wine and talk with my friend a bit more. There's a full moon, no mosquitoes, and this breeze is lovely."

ΦΦΦ

The next evening, Oleg had dinner on a client's dredge. Amorim stayed on his rig and Licco sought out Sandra's company once again. When she saw he'd come by himself, she sent Mariana off and the two old friends were alone together. She seemed more at ease and ready to open up.

"There are some things that can't be said in front of just anybody. Now I can tell you why I never went back to Manaus," Sandra began. "Well, except for the *garimpo*, where I'm feared and respected, everywhere else I'm the brunt of so much prejudice, because of my profession—even in superficial social exchanges. That's what it was like in Porto Velho and that's what it would be like back in Manaus. I'm going to remind you about some of my background and you'll understand. The Sandra Reis you knew was a happily married woman, who'd found her prince charming in Ricardo. They spent ten happy years together in Manaus, where they played lots of tennis, danced, had fun with their many friends. To make the couple's bliss complete, little Mariana was born and everything in their lives seemed to be going great. The baby wasn't even a year old when the prince had a massive heart attack during the night and was dead by morning. In a snap of the fingers, the princess found herself alone with a small child. His parents, who lived in Santa Catarina, invited her to live with them, so she spent a year selling everything she had in Manaus and getting ready for the move. That's when she met another man, and at first it seemed she would live another fairytale with him. Carried away by her emotions, she decided to stay where she was. She wrote her old in-laws, thanking them and informing them about her decision. She was happy again.

Someone abruptly turned up the volume in the nightclub, right underneath them, and they heard the voice of singer Gonzaguinha, telling them life is lovely—"*É a vida, é bonita, é bonita...*"

"I'll ask them to hold it down!"

"Don't," Licco said. "I love this song."

"*E não ter a vergonha de ser feliz*," Gonzaguinha sang on, admonishing the world not to be ashamed of happiness.

Sandra sighed and said nothing for a moment. Then she went on. "It wasn't long before I discovered the man was no prince. He was more like the worst species of frog. He drank a lot, and he'd lose control of himself and beat my daughter and me. It started happening rather regularly and yet I was simply passive. I felt immobilized, no strength or drive to react. I came to hate myself. By then we'd moved to Porto Velho, where he had some business, which wasn't going well. I tried to help him, but eventually my money ran out too and he started asking for my jewels—my only mementos of Ricardo, and I'd managed to hide them from him."

Sandra sat there motionless as the tears ran down her cheeks. In a few minutes she had regained her composure and resumed her story. "My makeup must look awful! Well, to make a long story short, the frog beat the princess so much that one day she passed out and when she woke up, she'd lost much of her ability to move, forever. Never again did she walk, dance, or play tennis. Her money was gone, and so were her friends. Still, she survived and even had some happiness. The biggest source was Mariana. She's more than a daughter. She's my protector, a true friend."

They were quiet for a while, as the music played on.

"This song sounds as if it had been written for Sandra Reis in the days of Ricardo. Today's Sandra doesn't have much in common with that carefree woman. I'll never set foot in Manaus again, where there are still a few friends who remember the princess I once was. That image belongs to me and as long as it lasts, I can stay strong and have the desire to go on living. I hope I can safeguard it forever. That depends upon your silence now, Licco. Will you promise it to me?"

"You can count on me, princess!"

They sat there without a word, listening to the last chords of music, each one deep in the past, recalling the good and bad times from their youth.

"*Mas isso não impede que eu repita. É a vida, é bonita, é bonita...*" But none of the hard times, Gonzaguinha sang, keep me from saying it again: life is lovely, life is lovely.

When the tune was over, someone put on Brazilian country music and Sandra told them to lower the volume downstairs.

"And you, Licco? I never did know how you and Berta ended up in Manaus."

"It's a long story, Sandra."

Licco felt a real need to share his past: his poor yet happy childhood in faraway Bulgaria, the persecution and almost miraculous rescue of Bulgarian Jews during World War II, his escape from a forced labor camp, and then crossing the Atlantic and his unexpected arrival in the Amazon in the company of Berta. He talked about Berta too, about how vital she had been to his happiness, about the void she had left.

Sandra listened in silence as her friend poured out his guts, telling the tale of his peripatetic life—his frustrations, his moments of sadness and joy, his uncertainties, and even some successes.

"Every single emigrant, especially the Jews who managed to escape the Holocaust, have unbelievable stories to tell," Licco went on. "In Manaus, I met a Mr. Schwartz, who had also survived the war. I know he was a good friend of Ricardo's, and sometimes he'd talk to us about his dramatic escape from Nazi Germany and how he made his way to Brazil. Just imagine: he went several days without food or drink, hidden inside the trunk of a car, until they crossed the German border into Switzerland. My brother David's story is fascinating too. He managed to escape from the labor camp in 1942, while I rotted away there for another year. I knew he'd joined the armed resistance that was fighting the fascist government. What I didn't know—and what he only told me recently—was that he was hunted down and captured by the Bulgarian police in June 1944, along with another young partisan, when they were committing an act of sabotage. They were both interrogated for hours. It was brutal, but they didn't utter a single word or give up any information about their comrades' hiding places. I find it remarkable how my brother recounts this chilling episode with a pinch of humor.

Since they weren't getting anywhere, their jailers resorted to the laws of physics—the most exact of the sciences—turning to Foucault's pendulum. Ever hear of it? They say it's a foolproof method for breaking down a stubborn prisoner. In the nineteenth century, a French scientist by the name of Foucault—I think it was Jean Bernard Foucault—observed that an absolutely motionless object hanging from a rope would slowly start rotating, accompanying the rotation of the earth. He could never imagine that decades later his notion would inspire fascist torturers, who created a type of human pendulum, hanging their victims upside down with their bare feet exposed. The position lent itself to myriad types of torture, which could easily be enhanced through the application of electric shocks—one bare wire wrapped around the big toe and the other end attached to some more sensitive part of the body. Forty years have passed and I still shudder at the thought; it makes me want to vomit. Sometimes I try to imagine how David could have taken it. Compared to him, I didn't suffer at all. And I think that compared to you, life has been easy on me as well."

It was getting hard for him to talk, but Licco struggled on. "David told me his feet were soon whipped to a bloody mush. After the first shocks, the so-called human pendulum starts peeing uncontrollably, and the warm liquid mixes with the blood and sweat and drips down your chest and neck, until big globs of it ooze into your mouth and nose."

Straining to control his emotions, Licco went on to tell how the men had eventually passed out and the two human wrecks had been dropped to the icy-cold floor of the cell—partly so their torturers could go home to dinner with their wife and children, as befits all respectable citizens. There'd be another session the next day, an even more productive one, and the jailers were certain their human pendulums would spill the beans. But that night, American and British planes bombarded the city of Sofia even harder than usual. A number of bombs hit one wing of the prison and a few felons managed to escape. The response had been to move all the prisoners to a smaller town, where the torture could not continue. Meanwhile, the Red Army had reached the Danube and the fascist power structure started crumbling. Judges, lawyers, district attorneys, investigators, torturers— people who had cooperated with the regime up until then—began playing dead. On September 9, 1944, the Red Army crossed the Danube and met with no resistance.

"That's how Oleg's father and many other souls were saved," Licco said. "In an ironic twist of fate, nearly thirty years later the poor fellow was arrested again, this time by the Communist regime, and falsely accused of espionage. Some day I'll tell you the second half of David's story. Because he had even taken up arms to defend his ideals, his second imprisonment was more painful and much more humiliating than Foucault's pendulum."

A very sleepy-faced Mariana came into the room to see how her mother was doing. It was approaching midnight. Licco got up. "Thanks for everything," he said. "I'll come say goodbye tomorrow. And I'll be back soon to see the dredge in operation, and then we can continue our conversation. It was wonderful to see you, Sandra."

"You too. We'll be at our new facilities in a month, in Palmeiral. That's where Oleg's dredge is too. I'd like to invite you to stay at my new hotel. When we have more time, I need to tell you some other tidbits about my life that you don't know—and I think you'll find them interesting. For now, Godspeed—and I'll look out for Russo."

They hugged each other long and hard. Words were no longer necessary. It was clear they could count on each other's solidarity and complicity.

ΦΦΦ

"I'm not exactly thrilled you're going into prospecting, but I realize there's nothing I can do about it. If you can't beat'em, join'em. That's how politicians approach things and that's what I'm going to do."

They were nearing Porto Velho and traffic was picking up.

"Uncle Licco, have faith in me and don't worry. Especially because Pounder and Sandra will be looking out for me."

"Pounder? Who's Pounder?"

Oleg chuckled as he drove down the road. He was pleased that the trip back was going smoothly, no accidents or incidents. The shadows of night were falling slowly and the lights of Porto Velho sparkled in the distance.

"Pounder is the nickname of our friend Amorim—because he's so scrawny, he can't weigh more than a pound! OK, so he weighs a bit more than that. But since he likes to give everybody else nicknames, he got a taste of his own medicine."

Licco had taken a firm liking to Amorim. He'd found him to be smart, levelheaded, and quite sensible—except when talking about his oldest son, his one single worry. Amorim's second oldest worked at the repair shop and the youngest was a rancher who managed the land where his family invested all its profits. The first time Licco heard Amorim complaining about his oldest, he immediately imagined the classic case of a ne'er-do-well or someone addicted to drugs or alcohol. He was taken aback when he found out what the real concern was.

"My son's in Scotland, at some university in Glasgow," Amorim had told him. "He went to college at the University of São Paulo, got his master's degree in the United States, and then his doctorate in Britain. He's 45 years old but he could care less about money, ranching, or anything else productive. The last time he came to visit me, he told me he's teaching medieval history. I have no clue what that's good for! Can you figure that? He's going to starve to death."

"Amorim, my friend, studying and teaching are very respectable things to do—maybe a rather big leap from the life we lead around here, but still, they're important to us all. Deep down you know that. Otherwise, why did you set up that library?" Licco hadn't been able to hide his smile. "Truth told, you should be proud of him."

Though Licco had failed to convince Amorim that there was any real point to his son's studies, the two men had parted good friends. Licco promised to bring some new books for the library and Amorim pledged to help his nephew out in his new endeavor.

Contrary to predictions, it took more than two months to get the dredge up and running. A number of minor things didn't work, or something would break down, as often is the case when machinery has sat unused for a long while. In late August, by which time the waters of the Madeira River had dropped much lower, Russo's dredge finally started up operations. Known as Suvaco da Velha, the site was not far from Palmeiral and was quite promising. Countless cascades interrupted the 250 miles of river running from Guajará-Mirim to Porto Velho, most of them separated by stretches of calm, navigable waters dozens of miles long. Hundreds of rigs crowded these spots, doing their best to avoid the gigantic tree trunks that would hurtle downstream and threaten to drag the vessels to the nearest waterfall. It was always a gamble.

For those living on the rigs, the future stretched no farther than the next separation of the gold from the gravel—the *despesca*. Hundreds of floats and dredges met their demise as immense logs dragged them under the roiling waters of Little Hill Falls or Hell's Caldron, the two biggest challenges in navigating the Upper Madeira, far outranking the eighteen other waterfalls and cascades. Formed from the meeting of the Mamoré and Beni rivers—the Mamoré longer but the Beni carrying more water—the great Madeira is easily navigable once it flows beyond Porto Velho. Hence the monumental push to build the Madeira-Mamoré railway in the late nineteenth century in order to transport rubber from Bolivia to Porto Velho without needing to negotiate the Madeira's perilous waterfalls. But the rubber boom ended right as the railway was inaugurated. Serving no purpose and thus left abandoned, most of the tracks had been eaten up by the forest over the following years, leaving only a short stretch to evoke the past days of glory.

In Porto Velho, Gabriel had taken over management of Berimex, replacing his boss and friend Oleg. Now he made frequent visits to the innumerable sites where promising *fofocas* were popping up all the time: Ímbauba, Prainha, Jirau, Palmeiral, Belmont, Periquito, Suvaco da Velha, and Ilha da Pedra, to name just a few.

Meanwhile, Russo—soon known to all by this name—drove headlong into recruiting a good crew that could spend at least one season working together. Employee turnover had to be avoided at all cost because it jeopardized the rig's round-the-clock operation. Moicano had been Amorim's helmsman for a good number of years and had also been a diver, and so when he offered to join up, Russo hired him immediately. Sandra found him a good cook, named Maria. Though she had been working temporarily at Sandra's restaurant, Maria had made it clear she'd rather be on a dredge, where the money was better. In exchange for five percent of the production—a likely twenty grams of gold a month—Maria agreed to cook, clean up around the rig, and do all the other general services. She made another ten grams a month washing and ironing her colleagues' clothes. Maria was a good-looking *cabocla*, tough yet cheerful, and she could have earned a lot more. There were plenty of prospectors who offered her ten or even fifteen grams of gold to enjoy an hour in her alluring arms but she always turned them down. Her adamant refusals and frosty stare scared off her sex-starved admirers. In their frustration, the would-be gallants labeled her frigid or called her a dyke, but everyone respected Russo's cook.

On the recommendation of acquaintances, Oleg hired two brothers who were experienced prospectors—Big Blackie and Little Whitie—and knew the region like the backs of their hands. In point of fact, Little Whitie was only a little lighter-skinned than his brother Big Blackie, but the difference had been enough to earn him the nickname. It was months before the whole crew was finally assembled. Its last addition was Antônio, an elementary school teacher turned prospector. He was a complete greenhorn who knew nothing about gold mining but proved to be a top-notch student. Less than a year later, he was already an expert. By combining luck with skill, and perfecting some production procedures, Russo's *despescas* were soon yielding over 200 grams—an outstanding figure. This good performance, topped by some incentives that he offered, made for a united, loyal crew.

Oleg found life on the dredge less tiring but more monotonous than he'd expected. The incessant sound of the engines was bothersome for the first several days, but those working on the dredge soon became aware of something interesting: despite the extremely loud noise, their attention was always drawn by any strange sound. The drop of a wrench or even of a coin stood out from the steady, regular hum of the engines and generator. Sleeping presented no problem. But you had to be careful not to fall in the water, especially at night, when the event might go unnoticed. There was also the constant threat of a tree trunk smashing into the rig, swept along by the muddy waters—accidents like this happened just about weekly. Once the anchors securing the floats and dredges had been yanked up, the vessel would be loose, out of control, and its neighbors would all be in peril. It was particularly dangerous in the vicinity of waterfalls or their churning whirlpools. More than one rig had been dragged away by the raging waters that drowned myriad dreams and many lives during those turbulent years.

Sandra and Amorim moved to Palmeiral the same week, in early September. The new nightclub was much nicer, the hotel roomier, and the brothel more welcoming. And the houseboat offered yet another essential service: a small but well-equipped pharmacy. It was a matter of keeping up with the competition. After all, at the many gold-mining villages along the river, a host of women of all ages, to please all tastes, plied their services for a few grams of gold.

Once everything was in place, Sandra insisted that Licco spend some more time on the Madeira, and Oleg asked Gabriel to get in touch with the Berimex office in Manaus.

A few days later, right during the *despesca*, a taxi boat docked at Oleg's dredge and two gentlemen got out, conspicuously overdressed for their environment. Gun in hand, Moicano warily watched their arrival, only lowering his weapon when he recognized one of them. It was Licco. The other fellow bore a great resemblance to him, except he was a bit balder.

"Put your guns away," shouted Oleg, who'd been covering Moicano. "It's my dad and uncle!" Their arrival was so unexpected that even the *despesca* was forgotten. Everybody wanted to meet Oleg's father, with whom he obviously shared a special relationship. The three men talked excitedly in Bulgarian while the rest of the crew went back to their usual tasks.

"Maria, lay out a feast!" Oleg instructed. "Grilled flagtail, fried manioc flour, black beans. Go heavy on the hot pepper, because we've been overrun by Bulgarians today. And a few cold ones wouldn't hurt either."

There was just one little hitch. While everybody was getting ready for dinner, Moicano sounded the alarm: a log was headed towards the dredge. Two more anchors were dropped in a rush and Big Blackie and Little Whitie raced off in a small motorboat to try to head off the damned torpedo. Their mission wasn't a total success but it was enough. The log gave the rig only a glancing blow and the anchors held tough. Everyone breathed a deep sigh of relief as the trunk disappeared in the dark. But the waters brushed another shadowy figure against the side of the dredge: the body of a dead man, yet another poor soul to vanish without a trace in the *garimpo*.

CHAPTER 5
SANDRA'S SECRETS

Those first few days, the Hazan brothers wanted to spend their time together on the dredge getting to know the gold-mining process from start to finish. But it wasn't long before Amorim and Sandra heard they'd arrived and summoned them to attend the so-called inauguration of the new nightclub, hotel, and pharmacy—the Nova Casa da Lola, which had already been doing a brisk business for a week or so. There was no saying no.

True to her word, Sandra assigned the brothers the finest suites in the place and saw to it that they were given the royal treatment. After their days on the dredge, it took a while to get back to an infinitely quieter world. In the beginning, it felt as if they were in a cathedral with a mighty echo, where everybody was shouting.

Sandra made it a point to introduce her protégées, including her two stars: Mocha Louca and Niara Nutbuster. Sandra's affection for her girls was visible, as was her protective attitude. But she also knew how to handle them. Licco had met some of them during his last trip, but David had no clue how to behave. Obeying orders, the girls kept a respectful distance and refrained from making any advances to the illustrious visitors. The inauguration boiled down to a fancy dinner, prepared by Maria, who had been called in for the occasion. A dozen dredge owners had also been invited, together with the special guests of the night, Licco, David, and Russo. Amorim showed up a bit later, in the company of two other men. It was easy to see they were his sons. They were much bigger and more muscular than their father but otherwise the resemblance was undeniable. Everyone knew Renato, the head mechanic at the shop, but the other face was new in the *garimpo*.

"My son Roberto," Amorim said. "A history professor in Scotland. I brought him along because I really wanted you to meet him, Licco."

Amorim wasn't sure what to expect after the introduction. Licco had defended the young intellectual when the two men had first met, but Amorim wondered if it hadn't been simply out of politeness. He was pleasantly surprised to see an animated conversation start up, not only with Licco but with Oleg and David as well.

"I spent my childhood and teenage years reading the books my father collected. I acquired a taste for literature, history, and geography and it's never left me. My father doesn't appreciate my profession. He thinks professors starve to death, but he's the main reason I made this choice. Besides, I'm single and I make enough to get by," Roberto said.

"A 45-year-old bachelor? I want grandkids—but

medieval history doesn't help that!" Amorim just couldn't get past it.

Then the fireworks started. A few small, strategically positioned motorboats lit up the sky around the hotel. Sandra did things up right! After dinner, the guests hurried back to their dredges and the restaurant could finally open its doors to the impatient customers. Sandra invited those who'd stayed behind to go upstairs to her personal quarters. It was a replay of what Licco had seen before: going up in the elevator moved by the muscle power of two strong men.

Sandra had pulled out all the stops. The top floor of the houseboat was spacious and even more elegant than her other one. After they'd all been given the grand tour, the inauguration came to its end—and Sandra asked to speak to Licco alone. He could sense she had something important to tell him.

Amorim and his sons got the message. When they were about to board their vessel home, Oleg's cook Maria asked for a ride; she had to work the next day. Oleg and David went to bed. Sandra sent her daughter away with a gesture, and the two friends were alone at last. Licco asked for a cigar and settled in to hear what Sandra had to say.

"I don't even know how to begin, my friend. No one knows the story I want to tell you. That includes Ricardo, my husband, may he rest in peace. I thought I'd take this story to my grave, but I feel I must respect my mother's wish that the whole truth be told. In any case, it won't really change anything.

"You knew me back in Manaus, when I was 25 or 26 and already married to Ricardo. According to my documents, I was born in Itacoatiara on June 11, 1924, the daughter of Ancelmo and Tamara Melo. I moved to Manaus with my mother when I was 10, shortly after my father died. He was a doctor. My mother lived another eight years. She caught tuberculosis and towards the end coughed so much she could barely talk. Months before she died, she started telling me some things from her childhood that I had known nothing about."

Sandra let out a deep sigh before continuing.

"She was born in a small village in the heart of Poland. That much of her story I'd known. My mother spoke Portuguese with a heavy accent even after living in Brazil for thirty years. She went on to tell me a little about life in Poland, about my grandparents, and then she started in on a strange story about her first marriage, back over in Europe. That was the first I'd heard anything about it. I always thought she'd been married just once, in Brazil, to my dad. When she started telling me about her honeymoon to South America, she got very upset and it got harder and harder for her to talk. She broke down crying and then said, 'Honey, I just can't get it out. It hurts too much, and it's a long story anyway. I'm going to try to write it all down. That way you won't have to try to remember certain names and events that profoundly marked my life and the lives of hundreds of other women.'

"From then on, she wrote for several hours every

day, and sometimes I'd catch her crying. I never asked her anything about our talk. When we're young, we're never in a hurry; we think we'll always have time for everything. I think I hadn't really paid much attention to the story, nor could I imagine my mother would die so soon. Then one morning, I didn't hear her coughing like she always did, and to my horror I discovered God had silently taken her while she was sleeping. One day, after the shock had passed, I found a bunch of papers and read them."

Her pause seemed to suggest that the most interesting part of the story was about to begin. Licco sat as still as he could.

"It was one surprise after the other. I simply hadn't known my mother. That's when I found out that her original name wasn't Tamara and that I had in fact been adopted. After I had read the manuscript a second time, I stuck it away in a folder and tried to forget it. The only reason I didn't throw it out was because my mother had insisted the tale be told some day. I read it again after I'd been confined to this wheelchair, and again last week. That's when I decided to choose you as my confidant and ask you a favor. I'd like you to arrange for the tombs of my mother and of Sara Rosales to be cleaned; they lie next to each other. It'll be easy to find them at São João Batista Cemetery, near the entrance to the Jewish Cemetery in Manaus. Who knows, maybe some day, after this story has been told, the community will decide to take care of the tombs of the other people involved."

"Of course." Licco broke his own silence. "What community are you referring to?"

Ignoring the question, Sandra went on. "The story's so long I'd rather tell it tomorrow, when we'll have more time. Today I've got another matter for dessert. I need the benefit of your experience and some advice on how to deal with a tremendous headache, a problem that's troubling someone you know and someone I care a great deal about."

"Who are you talking about, Sandra? I know so few people around here." Licco was perplexed.

"I'm talking about Maria—Maria Bonita—Oleg's cook. She worked in my restaurant for a few years and I really like her, and trust her. She has three children: Isaías, who's going to medical school in São Paulo; Alice, who just got her business degree; and Lídia, who's still studying journalism. Not bad for a humble cook who works in the *garimpo*. Of course this has cost a lot in gold and it's going to take still more. That's why I let her go, so she could work for your nephew. On the dredge, as part of a prospecting crew, she earns a lot more, but she also renders another service—she's in charge of looking out for Oleg and, if necessary, protecting him."

"You've got to be kidding, Sandra!" Licco could hardly believe his ears. "Oleg was an officer in the Army and he fought in a war. I don't think he needs a nanny! A cook looking out for him? Only if she's looking out for his stomach!"

"Here in the *garimpo*, my dear friend, everybody needs a guardian angel. You don't know Maria Bonita. Of course she does an excellent job taking care of food and clothes for the prospectors on the dredge, which is by far the cleanest, tidiest in the *garimpo*. But believe it or not, Maria the *cabocla* is also an excellent marksman. Besides, she's the friend of someone who wants what's best for your nephew. That person is Sandra, who once was a good tennis player. And who talks to Maria Bonita every day. Have you got it now?"

"You amaze me. I have noticed Maria. First of all, because of that unbeatable tambaqui she makes better than anyone else. Second, because of her green eyes and how she's just so plain nice to everyone. She's a real sweet person. I just couldn't imagine she was your lookout."

"Sweet, decent, and plucky," Sandra drove home. "I know it's late but I want to tell you her story, so you can understand why I've picked you to turn to for advice. When I sent Maria to work on the dredge, I figured one day she'd tell Oleg everything and ask for his advice, but she's too shy for that. So I'm going to tell the story myself."

Speaking slowly and softly, the elderly woman began her account of the life of the *cabocla* Maria from her time on the distant Purus River to her tragic departure from Quatro Ases.

"So Alice isn't the daughter of Maria Bonita and Adriano, but of Nina and Benjamin Melul," Licco said.

"I used to know some of the Meluls way back when, in Manaus, but I haven't seen any of them in ages. They must have moved to Rio de Janeiro. There are a bunch of folks from the Amazon who attend Shel Guemilut Hassadim synagogue. It shouldn't be hard to find them."

"Precisely. But how do we explain what Maria's kept hidden all these years? In the eyes of a misguided judge, she's committed a crime, even if Alice does consider Maria her mother and Isaías and Lídia, her siblings. Alice knows a bit about her background, especially the fact that she's of Jewish descent. Maria kept Benjamin's prayer books and taught her to light the candles at sundown every Friday. But that's all she knows about the Jewish religion."

"My God, Sandra. What a mess. The things that have taken place in the immense Amazon forest simply astound me--out here, in the boondocks of the ends of the earth! I'd never had direct contact before but I'd heard tell of descendants of Italians, Portuguese, Arabs, and Jews who for some reason had wandered away from their roots and came to color the palette here in the heart of the Amazon, nothing but *caboclos* now. Where's this girl? I wouldn't be able to give you any reasonable advice without talking to her and Maria."

"Maria and Alice hid the facts from the whole world," Sandra went on. "Until recently, Maria was getting a lot of help from former Governor Jorge Teixeira and especially from his wife Aída. They met when the governor was visiting Fortaleza de Abunã, and then Maria worked as a cook at their home for several years."

"I met Teixeirão—Big Teixeira, as they called him—when he was head of the Military College in Manaus." Licco took great pride in his friendship with the legendary officer. "He was elected mayor and was the best our capital had seen in ages. He was quite the athlete. We used to play volleyball Sundays in the sand court at the Bosque Club. I remember well when he was appointed governor of the former Federal Territory of Rondônia in 1979, with the mission of making it into a State."

"And the Teixeirão era in Rondônia ended just a couple years back, in 1985," Sandra added. "He was the first governor of the new State. Maria was really lucky to have won him over and gained his help. Without this advantage, being all alone in the world, she never would have managed to give her three children the comfortable life and good education they've had. Colonel Teixeira could have been a great help straightening out the question of Alice's true identity, but Maria never brought the matter up to him. She was afraid they'd take the girl from her, and neither she nor Alice wanted that. That's why everyone today believes Alice is the daughter of Maria and the late Adriano Antunes."

"Sandra, honestly, looking at this from the outside, and not knowing all the facts, I think it might be better to just leave things lie. Unless there's some kind of inheritance involved. Does Alice want the truth to come out?"

"Not exactly. It's Maria, who was like a sister to Nina Melul, who has regrets. There's the matter of the girl's faith. Perhaps as Jews, you and your family might have an idea here. I really like Maria. I owe her a lot, and I'd like to pay her back. Please help me, Licco."

"I'll have a talk with Oleg and my daughter Sara too. She's a judge, so she'll be knowledgeable about the legal implications. But first I need to talk to Maria and her daughter. I promise you we'll find the least traumatic solution."

"Thank you, my friend. We'll have to talk more about this, but that's enough for today. Tomorrow night I'll tell you my mother's story, which is another shocker—a veritable atom bomb. Good night, Licco."

Licco went back to his room a little dizzy from the alcohol, the Cuban cigar, and Sandra's revelations.

"Life plays too many tricks on us," he thought as he drifted to sleep. "And I had to come here to the *garimpo* to hear these stories…! Sandra's Polish mother, the *cabocla* Maria Bonita, and her Jewish daughter. Real life is much more astonishing than anything the human imagination could dream up."

ΦΦΦ

The day rushes by in the *garimpo*. Licco and David went out to visit some of the villages along the river and reached Oleg's dredge at lunchtime. The roar of the machinery seemed even more deafening than before.

After their meal, Licco went to talk to Maria Bonita. He cut straight to the chase, telling Maria about his conversation with Sandra the night before. The green eyes that had stolen the heart of the *caboclo* Adriano filled with tears. He could barely hear her soft voice above the noise of the machines as she choked out a few words. Licco hadn't realized he was clumsily invading Maria's privacy, and now it seemed he'd stabbed her to the core. "So Sandra told you. The time has come for me to pay for my mistakes."

"No, that's not it at all! I'd like to talk with you and your daughter somewhere else, more private. Trust me. I want to help you both."

"I'm going to spend a few days with my daughters in Porto Velho starting next Friday. Could we meet there?"

Licco immediately agreed. The stop would be convenient for him since he and David would be going back to Manaus that Sunday. They could have a nice long talk.

"Let's all go to Porto Velho together on Friday," Licco suggested. "Oleg is taking us in his pickup. Are we all set then?" Maria nodded.

A while later, when Licco was getting into the boat to head back to the hotel, he waved goodbye to Maria and she returned the wave. She looked more at ease. Perhaps she was even relieved more people knew her secret.

"She's always so helpful, so kind—and just such a

sweetheart," Licco thought. "And she's still attractive. She must have been beautiful when she was young."

The night held other revelations, and even more surprising ones. Licco soon understood why Sandra had compared her mother's story to an atom bomb. Sandra had invited David to sit in on their conversation, and he had to work hard even to get the gist of the story. His knowledge of Portuguese came through Ladino, or Judeo-Spanish, the language spoken by the Jews who were expelled from the Iberian Peninsula by the Inquisition in the late fifteenth century. They had taken it with them to northern Africa, the Ottoman Empire, and Holland. He could understand simple conversations, but Tamara Melo's story demanded much more. Still, David knew that important things were being said, and he could sense it whenever Sandra was overcome with emotion. He didn't interrupt by asking questions; Licco would explain later.

"After I've told you my mother's story, I'm going to give you the manuscript so you can find somewhere safe to keep it." Sandra showed him a thick ream of papers filed away in a folder. "Some day someone might want to know a little more about the tragic fates she describes. These papers are to be made public only after my death, and without revealing the author's true name. To protect me and my descendants, the names Tamara and Ancelmo Melo are not mentioned anywhere; my mother used fictitious names. There's no worry about revealing the other names and facts. After you've read it all, you'll realize my mother was a wise woman. She completely spared me from any contact with this history."

"As I said earlier," Sandra went on, "Tamara wasn't her original name. Her real name was Rifca Blumenfeld. She was born in 1887 in a tiny Polish village not far from Bełżyce, near the Russian border. Everyone in the village was Jewish, they all spoke Yiddish, and only a few of them knew any Polish."

"My God, you're Jewish! I always thought you were Catholic, like Ricardo." Licco couldn't believe it.

"I am Catholic. I was raised Catholic. My parents wanted as much distance as possible between me and my mother's past. You'll understand once you've heard her whole story."

Sandra took a sip of guaraná soda and continued.

"My mother said practically everyone—save the butcher—was poor. They led simple lives. Rabbi Zalman was a kind and just man who wisely settled all disputes. Besides their poverty, their biggest nightmare were the pogroms that occasionally took place and that everyone regarded as a kind of inevitable fatality, like an earthquake or flood. Because of the pogroms, married women kept pregnant all the time, so they wouldn't get pregnant during the inevitable rapes. The problem was the young single women, the biggest victims of this violence. The Blumenfeld girls had escaped by a hair during some of the Cossack invasions, hidden away in a tiny, stinky lean-to, next to the cesspit, and they were well aware of the horrors that transpired. They and their girlfriends dreamt of having the chance to go to America one day."

Sandra paused for a little more soda and then resumed her story.

"Solomon and Rebeca Blumenfeld had three daughters. Rifca was the oldest, followed by Esther, one year younger, and Raquel, the baby. When Rifca was 15, Rebeca suddenly took ill and died just two weeks later. After he'd recovered from the shock, Solomon looked for another wife. Despite the best efforts of Seidele the matchmaker, it was only two years later, when Mordecai the baker passed away, that his widow, Miriam, became a possible candidate—actually, the lone candidate. In an instant, the family grew, with Miriam contributing two sons from her first marriage. Around the same time, something happened in the tiny village that affected the lives of almost every single inhabitant. As my mother tells it, on a particularly cold, gray Friday in the Polish autumn while everyone was getting ready for synagogue, a carriage pulled by two splendid horses stopped in the small central square and two dapper young men climbed out. The carriage was splattered with mud and the horses were exhausted, but the young men were impeccably and stylishly dressed. A little later, after synagogue, the talk of the town was that the two well-groomed young men were prosperous Jewish businessmen from Buenos Aires who were looking for young maidens to wed. Seidele, the matchmaker, just about went nuts! She started drawing up a list of the names of girls between the ages of 15 and 22. In keeping with tradition and good manners, the visitors sought out the rabbi. They introduced themselves in perfect Yiddish and showed Rabbi Zalman their documents. No, they weren't looking for wives but for young women to work as governesses in wealthy Jewish homes in Argentina. Business aside, yes, they were bachelors who had the best intentions and would like to meet some pretty, virtuous maidens, perhaps to take in marriage.

"Back then, Argentina was a rich nation and one of the favorite destinations of the Jews who were fleeing Eastern Europe en masse, especially the pogroms of Poland and Russia. In their desperation, people often overlooked the dangers, casting caution to the wind. As in many other shtetls, everyone believed firmly in the promise of a better life in far-off South America. Once a daughter had set up housekeeping in that paradise, she could help her whole family get out of Poland. To make a long story short, over the protests of Rabbi Zalman, Rifca married one of the illustrious visitors days later in a *stille chuppah*, a rushed, improvised marriage not presided over by a rabbi. Two weeks after their triumphant arrival, the two nice young men left the village in the company of the happy bride and some other girls, headed to the port of Marseilles."

"Zwi Migdal!" said Licco in horror, recognizing the ploy. "Atrocious! I've read a lot about them. They were an organized crime group that attracted hundreds of young Jewish women with promises of marriage or a well-paid job in the Americas. As I recall, the group started up in 1860 and was still going in 1939. The women were illiterate, penniless, and couldn't speak the local language. They had no friends, and no hope. They were forced into prostitution right on the boat over. Many were beaten, and raped as virgins. They were truly white slaves. The girls were treated so shamefully that the search for new recruits was called 'remounting'—a term that means to get a new horse for a rider."

"As always, Licco, you are well informed. My mother was one of those unfortunate women: a Pollack, as the Polish prostitutes were known."

"I've heard about them being here in the Amazon. If I'm not mistaken, they sometimes made donations to the synagogue in Manaus back then, even though they couldn't step foot in the door," Licco replied.

"Most of them stayed on in Argentina, according to my mother. There was a sharp disparity in the country at the close of the nineteenth century: nearly ten men for every woman, so sex-trafficking was an extremely profitable business. But the Zwi Migdal mafia was active in Brazil as well. There were Pollacks in Porto Alegre, Santos, São Paulo, Rio de Janeiro, Belém, and Manaus. In the early twentieth century, Manaus and Belém were extremely wealthy towns and demand was high on those markets."

Licco remembered some noteworthy facts. "In Buenos Aires and Rio de Janeiro, the so-called Pollacks founded their own synagogues and associations so they could honor their religious traditions and remain Jewish. Since they weren't accepted by society, they couldn't attend traditional synagogues or even be buried in Jewish cemeteries. You see evidence of this at Inhaúma Cemetery in Rio de Janeiro, where there are hundreds of markers not only of Pollacks but a few pimps as well. Since society refused to accept them even after they'd died, they founded the Israelite Funeral and Religious Charity Association just so they could have a dignified death, even after a wretched life."

"A lot of people associate Jews with wealth, banks, financial institutions, and precious gems and jewelry," Licco pointed out, "but the truth of the matter is that over the past five thousand years, no other people has had so much experience with poverty, slavery, pogroms, racial prejudice, and hatred—and then there were the Inquisition and Holocaust as well. Over the course of history, we've had to shed many tears as a people. Ergo the saying: tears dry up but the salt remains. And it wasn't just a little salt! In response to these persecutions and tough lives, we've been forced to study and devote ourselves to work more and more. That's why so many of us have become great doctors, philosophers, actors, filmmakers, painters, musicians, writers, businessmen, and scientists. Look how many Nobel prizes: almost one-fifth of the award-winners have Jewish roots. First and foremost, this is the product of hard work and sacrifice."

"My mother's story is far from over," Sandra said. "She goes into painstaking detail describing the arrival of nearly twenty young Jewish girls in Manaus in 1906. She lists the original names of every single one and the names they adopted in Brazil. Then she tells about their early days and their adaptation to the hot and humid Amazon. She recounts the fantastic story of Rabbi Shalom Muyal, who died in Manaus in 1910 and is worshipped as a saint by the local population, who continue to stop by his grave when hoping for a miracle. Using false names to protect privacy, she writes about her courtship with the young, poor Ancelmo Melo and how she supported him for years while he studied medicine, eventually graduating from the Pará School of Medicine. Were it not for the happy ending, it would have been one more case of a besotted woman sacrificing herself for her beloved. Dr. Melo went back to Manaus, but out of gratitude, or love, or perhaps both, he did marry the Pollack Rifca, who at that point was called Tamara. The happy couple moved to the town of Itacoatiara, where no one knew her, and there they led a calm and peaceful life. Mrs. Melo became a *grande dame* of local society. She was Catholic like her husband; she did philanthropic work and made generous contributions to the church. The couple couldn't have children, but in 1925 something intriguing happened. One day, an elegant young woman disembarked at the port of Itacoatiara carrying a baby just a few days old. Sara Rosales, a Pollack well known in Manaus, went to the home of Dr. Ancelmo Melo, and when she went back to the port for the return trip to Manaus, the baby was no longer with her. That child, my dear Licco, was me. Sara Rosales is my real mother's name." She could barely get the words out but the tears came readily.

"What an amazing story. I've heard about another Pollack, Lola, who ran a very famous house in Manaus at the height of the rubber boom. She raised the children of her so-called protégées at a nursery school far away from the brothel. There weren't any efficient birth control methods back then, so of course the poor things had children, and rarely were their fathers known. The story goes that on her death bed, Lola tried to return to Judaism and so she left all her assets to the community. In exchange, she wanted the right to a Jewish burial and a Jewish tombstone. Since she couldn't live as a Jew, she was adamant that she'd be one after her death."

Sandra had regained her composure. She smiled. "Where do you think the name of my business here in the *garimpo* comes from: Casa da Lola?"

ΦΦΦ

The trip to Porto Velho took several hours. Oleg drove carefully; the road was dangerous and extremely slippery in spots. Only when they drew closer to the city was it blacktopped. They hardly spoke, each of the passengers deep in their own concerns. Oleg was transporting the gold gathered over the course of several days and he wanted to get rid of it as soon as possible. The others in the truck had no clue of the danger they were in. David, who had never heard of Zwi Migdal before, was still trying to process Tamara Melo's story. Maria was anxiously imagining Alice's reaction when she found out that the conversation that night would decide her fate. Licco couldn't stop thinking of Berta and his eternal friend Salvator; now that he had some important decisions to make, it would be essential to know their opinions.

They had to wait for the ferry to take them across the Madeira River to the city, where they headed at last to the house where Maria's daughters lived. They arranged to meet back up later in the day. Maria grabbed her belongings and said goodbye.

Towards the end of the afternoon, Licco and David were waiting in the lobby of the Vila Rica Hotel when the three women walked in, right on time. Oleg had gone out to sell their most recent gold earnings and hadn't returned yet. Licco didn't want to delve into the matter at hand without him there. Meanwhile, he wanted to get to know the girls. It wasn't hard to guess which one was Lídia. She had the same green eyes as her mother, the same lithe figure, and even a similar voice. Alice was totally different. It was hard to define the color of her eyes; she was shorter and gave the impression of being fragile and defenseless. Then David said something in Ladino, which sounded funny when heard through Brazilian ears, and everybody laughed. Licco was struck to see the same dimples on Alice's face that had charmed him about Berta over forty years earlier, on the train to Istanbul.

"Unbelievable. Even though there's no relationship, Alice looks remarkably like Berta when she was young, and Lídia took after her mother completely," he thought.

The meal was the last thing that mattered about that tense, decisive dinner. When Oleg finally arrived, they ordered food from the hotel restaurant, which was practically empty. They exchanged some polite social amenities and then it was time for the topic they were all anxiously waiting for. Maria was visibly tense, but Alice and Lídia seemed quite at ease. Licco took the initiative. "First, I want to express my immense pleasure in enjoying the company of three *hermosas* women, as David would say. Second, before we get down to business, I want to make it very clear that we have to find a solution that satisfies the main interested party, Alice."

Clearly anxious, Maria spoke up right away. "Alice, Lídia, and I had a talk this afternoon. Alice would like to leave things as they are. She doesn't want to change anything."

Speaking calmly and decidedly, Alice explained, "For twenty years, Maria has been my mother and only God knows how much she's sacrificed to raise us. I hardly remember my parents. All that's left of them are those prayer books in Hebrew, a language I don't even know. The only book I can read is *Ethics of our Fathers*. While I believe in God, I haven't followed any formal religion in all my 23 years. All that aside, I'm

145

Maria's daughter. Isaías and Lídia are my brother and sister."

Licco listened without saying a word. As he watched the girl declare her love for her mother and siblings, he felt like he was watching a movie. He could feel that David and Oleg were moved, and he saw that Maria was holding back tears.

"I'm not even going to talk to Sara," thought Licco. "Maria's doubts aside, these three women are happy, and there's nothing to be done. If Berta and Salvator were here with me, they'd agree."

Oleg spoke up. "I can help you learn a bit about the Jewish religion and traditions. They reflect our greatest legacy: the cultural experience we've accumulated over five thousand years. You have a right to this heritage."

"Where? In the *garimpo*? I don't like it there; I can't stand that lifestyle and I'd love to get my mother to leave."

Licco nearly broke into applause. This apparently fragile, vulnerable girl was quite sure of herself, and she challenged Oleg as naturally as could be. He'd finally met his match.

"I'll be coming to Porto Velho next Friday. We always celebrate the Sabbath at my friends' house, and I'd like to take you with me so you could get to know a bit more about our traditions."

"It would be my great pleasure. But just remember, I'm Alice Antunes, creature of the wild, born on the Abunã River, daughter of Maria Bonita and grand-

146

daughter of a green-eyed dolphin," she announced proudly, and Licco once again wanted to applaud.

The conversation was over. Oleg went to drop the three women back home while the two brothers went to the hotel bar.

"I'm going to have a glass of champagne. I think Oleg has found his muse!" David exclaimed. "I find Alice absolutely charming and I think he does too."

"I really liked both girls. Lídia looks a bit like a model, and Alice reminds me of Berta when she was young. Her eyes seem to have their own light. She knows exactly what she wants, and I'm going to pray for her to include my nephew on her list. David, you need some grandchildren fast!" The brothers laughed hard.

"Looks like Maria Bonita's problem has been solved faster and better than we could have hoped. Let's hope Alice can soon solve ours!"

CHAPTER 6
THE PRAINHA WAR

Early in the week, after several continuous hours of suctioning the riverbed and separating out the gold, the whole crew realized something different was going on. They turned off the engine, started beating the carpets, and a shower of sparkling flecks of metal rained down. As experienced prospectors, they knew they'd hit it big. Gold is found in the form of nuggets elsewhere but on the Madeira River, it comes in the form of fine particles of metal mixed in with other minerals. When mercury is added, it sticks to the gold and forms a ball. When subjected to high temperatures, the mercury quickly evaporates, leaving pure gold as its final product.

The dredge produced an incredible 560 grams of gold that day and everybody's satchels were soon stuffed with the metal. The two smaller dredges that accompanied Oleg's—Cabeção's and Chico Paraíba's—also had a very productive day. The dredges would usually position themselves in groups so they could help each other out when necessary. It was also a way of protecting themselves against the bands of thieves that often attacked the more vulnerable rigs.

They stayed in the same location for two more days and continued to hit pay dirt. On the fourth day, Moicano and Maria went off to buy fuel and provisions. When they got back in the late afternoon, Maria went straight to talk to Oleg.

"Dona Sandra asked me to warn you to keep your eyes open. One of Chico Paraíba's workers spent a few hours at her nightclub and spread the news that we struck it rich. By now, there must be a hundred dredges planning to prospect in our area. Two or three days from now, we're sure to have a lot of company. And one of the girls heard from a customer that the Bolivian gang is near Palmeiral and cooking up a big attack. Dona Sandra is afraid they're going to hit us. Especially now that everybody knows we've hit pay dirt. She's so worried she's sending us a motorboat today with arms and ammunition. Amorim promised to help too. He asked Gabriel to notify the police. I sent news to Alice and Lídia that we won't be visiting them this weekend."

Oleg knew he didn't have much time to prepare to defend the dredges. First thing he had to do was let everybody know they wouldn't have any breaks over the next few days. With their bags stuffed with gold, some of the crew were eager to go out on the town and drown their sorrows in the arms of some fiery *cabocla*. With all that gold, the gals would be lined up. These plans would have to be delayed.

Still, things weighed in the prospectors' favor. Their enemy was counting on the element of surprise and couldn't imagine they were the ones in for a surprise. Oleg had to draw up a good plan of defense and pray that the reinforcements got there fast. First he went to talk to Chico Paraíba and Cabeção, bosses of the other rigs. Everyone was in agreement that if they were attacked, they had to stand their ground. The other option would have been to abandon the dredges and just wait and see. But that really wouldn't work. In their frustration, the invaders would no doubt destroy all the equipment or cut the anchor cables so the dredges would float away and break apart over the next whitewater rapids. The prospectors would sustain tremendous losses. On the other hand, they had an urgent need for reinforcements. Oleg didn't have many hands on board for a good defense: just twelve men and three women.

They arranged to have two men stand guard around the clock. At nightfall, two motorboats would position themselves a ways away from the dredges and try to spot any intruders in the dark. This was vital because the roar of the engines was so deafening that you couldn't hear a thing inside the rigs and you wouldn't have enough advance warning if any evil-doers were to approach. It was also crucial that the equipment stay running so everything would look normal. Yet another urgent task: instead of dumping the gravel back into the river, they would use it to build small barricades to afford those on the dredges additional protection. The only other thing would be to pray that the attack wouldn't be that same night, before reinforcements arrived.

Oleg knew that with so little lead time he couldn't expect much help from the fledgling state government's underequipped and poorly trained police, but still, it was important to advise them. So Gabriel's assistance was most welcome. By letting the authorities know what was afoot, it would make it that much easier to explain the episode later, especially if there were any deaths.

It was a long but peaceful night. Even so, no one managed to sleep. At the first sign of light, Oleg began keeping an eye on the movement of boats in the vicinity and carefully studying the edge of the river, armed with a pair of binoculars. The place was known as Prainha— Little Beach—but the waters of the Madeira River were rising, and the beach, which was quite long in the dry season, had simply disappeared. It didn't seem very likely that anyone would attack from that direction but the possibility couldn't be discarded out of hand. Flat-bottomed motorboats could indeed move in on them from the beach side. So Oleg decided to position some shooters in the woods up on the riverbank. It was a great vantage point. From there, they could offer protection if the attack came from the beach; in fact, they could do major damage to the aggressors no matter which way they came from. But their own numbers were just so few.

The attack would most likely come at night, when the dredges were all lit up and the world around them pitch black. And the odds would be stacked in favor of the invaders. They would be able to move in quite close without being noticed, while the roaring machines masked any sound outside. On the other hand, the defenders would be bathed in bright light and unable to see the intruders, hidden under cover of darkness.

"Lighting! Lighting might be our salvation."

The dredges had powerful spotlights but they wouldn't be enough. This type of maritime light can only stay on for short periods, just so the helmsman can get his bearings. Then it has to be turned off and only turned on again a while later. A different solution was needed. Then Maria Bonita came up with an idea.

"Dona Sandra always keeps a stock of fireworks. She shoots them off on New Year's Eve, Carnival, and Independence Day. She used some a while back, for the inauguration of the hotel. They draw people from all over the *fofoca*, and then her girls bring in more money."

That would be the solution. It was still morning, and there'd be enough time for Moicano to get the fireworks and return. Oleg went over to Alemão's dredge, which was not very far away. He told him what was going on and asked for his help.

Now all they had to do was wait, and act normal, as if no one were imagining an imminent attack.

The day flew by in the blink of an eye. The first reinforcements arrived: two bouncers from Sandra's, loaded with arms and ammunition. A little while later, everyone was surprised when Roberto, the professor of medieval history, showed up with three other fellows.

"Where's your armor, pal?" Oleg teased him.

"I've got some for you too," Roberto joked back,

showing Oleg a pile of bulletproof vests in the bottom of his canoe.

The dredges belonging to Alemão and his buddies couldn't move fast enough to arrive in time. Instead, they sent a canoe with two well-armed men to provide immediate help. Later that day, from the second floor of his suction dredge, Oleg raised his binoculars and watched with growing concern as an unusually large number of motorboats began circulating on the other side of the river. More than ten vessels were moving in and there were probably more that he couldn't see.

"Sandra's right. It's going to be here. And it's going to be tonight," Oleg thought. "To judge from the motor-boats, there must be at least thirty gunmen. They're expecting to face fifteen of us, tops, and they're also counting on the element of surprise. A surprise is what they're going to get!"

In the late afternoon, Oleg assembled his troops—by that time, twenty men and three women—and assigned each one a specific task. The fireworks were divided into three lots: one load at water level, hidden in the woods in a nearby cove; another atop the riverbank; and a bigger load on the second floor of the dredge. Roberto and the three women were supposed to set off rockets and spray gunfire from the riverbank, as if a veritable battalion were up there. Likewise on land but hidden in the cove, two men had express orders to fire rockets towards the invaders as soon as the first shot was fired. It was essential that the tasks be carried out precisely, since this could have a decisive influence on the battle's outcome. The gunmen, especially those on the top floor of the dredge, would be at a great advantage if their targets were in bright light. The improvised gravel barricades were ready; there was even one on the second floor. So the stage was set. The minutes dragged by, and in the blackness of night, time seemed to stand still. If anyone present had been a stranger to anxiety, the feeling was now an intimate friend.

Midnight came and went. A thick cloud layer kept any heavenly light from reaching the earth. Then, at around two in the morning, a shot rang out from atop the riverbank and a rocket tore through the night. That same instant, the engines on the dredges fell silent, their interior lights went out, and spotlight beams burst through the dark. A succession of fireworks bathed the muddy waters of the Madeira River in an explosion of light. This was followed by a hailstorm of gunfire from all directions. The brief period of clarity allowed them to clearly see a dozen motorboats slowly advancing towards the dredges. But the roles had suddenly been reversed. Now the dredges were in the dark and the motorboats in the light, sitting ducks. Caught unawares, some of the boats did manage to change direction and take shelter in the safety of darkness, but others were already too close and had no time to flee. To add to the confusion, one helmsman had taken a direct hit and tumbled over into the water, and his motorboat kept going in circles. Completely out of control, it hit another boat and both vessels spit their passengers into the river. Before they could figure out what had gone wrong, five gunmen had been captured and tied up.

For a moment, silence hung in the air. Then someone up on the riverbank shot off one last rocket—this time to celebrate victory. The Prainha War was over.

Much later that morning, the bodies of four gunmen were found floating in the water some miles downstream. Amorim offered to pick them up and bury them once the police had completed their work, but during the following night someone—probably annoyed by the smell of decomposing bodies—pushed the corpses back into the strong current, where they disappeared in the churning rapids.

The police got there only two days later, by which time most of the weapons had been hidden away and all that was to show for it were some old shotguns. The police chief, who had heard one tall tale too many in his life, didn't ask many questions, and simply left with the five prisoners and the corpse of the dead helmsman.

"Bolivians my foot! Those fellows were Brazilians. I know the dead one. They call him Fatso," the police chief declared.

Fatso owned some dredges in the Jirau *garimpo* and was a well-known figure. Many prospectors had accused him of being the ringleader of the gang and financing attacks on other dredges, but nothing had ever been proven. Now there was no room for doubt. Oleg remembered seeing a fat man when he and Gabriel had been ambushed on the road to Porto Velho. It was probably the same thug, but he couldn't be sure.

If Russo had been well known and respected before the Prainha War, now his fame spread ever farther and wider through the *fofocas*. The rough prospectors revered this man who had defied an enemy that far outnumbered his own troops and had won the battle without sustaining a single casualty. His victory was credited to his leadership skills and his experience as an officer in the Israeli Army—and the size of the confrontation was greatly exaggerated by rumor. Oleg had become the most renowned and admired man not only in Palmeiral but along the entire Madeira River.

"Russo, you don't have any more excuses. Alice and Lídia are expecting us this weekend," Maria reminded him.

CHAPTER 7

OLEG AND ALICE

Oleg and Maria reached Porto Velho after a long, exhausting trip, all of it driving through a heavy downpour that turned the road into a bog. They exchanged hardly a word. The storm itself added tension to the air, but it was also as if each one were lost in his own thoughts. Oleg was seriously worried; he not only had to exchange the nearly 65 Troy ounces of gold from the last beating of the carpets and deposit the money—he'd have to find some investment that would protect the value of this hard-earned product. He didn't know which scared him the most: thieves or a monetary investment gone sour.

Inflation was skyrocketing, people felt downhearted, and nobody claimed to be a proud "citizen officer" in President Sarney's program to enforce a price freeze anymore; his monetary plan was a flop, and it was essentially every man for himself. If you kept your cash at home, you were poorer in days. Speculation led to unpredictable and sometimes unthinkable situations. Like all Brazilians, Oleg was extremely worried about things. He was frightened about whether the country's return to

democracy would hold firm and about possible compli-
cations stemming from the fact that Sarney hadn't been
directly elected to his post—instead, as vice-president-
elect, he had been sworn into office after Tancredo
Neves, the president-elect, fell ill; Neves then died one
month later, before being sworn into office himself.
Brazil faced enormous challenges and no one had defined the priorities for a country deep in crisis. When
Maria invited Oleg in for a cup of coffee before he
headed to his hotel, Oleg seemed to awake from a deep
sleep. He accepted her invitation.

He didn't expect Maria to live in such a large,
roomy home, and in a prime location. It didn't seem like
an affordable place for a cook from the *garimpo*. Alice
and Lídia each had her own room and so did Camila, a
sweet, cheerful teenager he hadn't ever met.

"I didn't know you had another daughter, Maria,"
Oleg remarked.

"Camila's not really my daughter, but she's like one
to me," Maria replied without further explanation.
"She'll sleep with me tonight, and you can have her
room. It's too late for you to be out on the streets transporting so much gold."

There was no way to refuse. Truth be told, Oleg was
delighted. The food was delicious and he was the center
of attention. They didn't run out of topics. Maria and
the girls wanted to know all about him and they show-
ered him with questions. He was hesitant at first, but as
he grew surer of himself, he ended up telling them

about his happy childhood in Bulgaria, about the Cold War, his parents' separation, and the unjust sentencing of his father David, accused of treason and espionage by the very Communist government that he had helped to build. He described the tough years following his father's arrest and their cinematic flight through the Iron Curtain, with the help of Licco and Berta. He also told them how Israel had welcomed him, about his stress-filled years in the Army, and, at last, his coming to Brazil.

When he had finished, a brief silence fell.

"I thought we'd been through hard times, but I see you've had your share as well." Maria saw her boss in a completely new light now.

"The only thing I don't understand is why you decided to go to the *garimpo*. Could you tell us?" Alice asked.

"I don't even really know myself. I think I wanted to prove to everyone—particularly to me—that I could earn a living without anybody else's help."

"There are so many better things a man with your background could do," Alice argued.

"Maybe I haven't made a lot of money in the *garimpo*, but the *garimpo* is how I met all of you," Oleg said, looking for an honorable way out.

"We heard about the so-called Prainha War. What madness!" Lídia said with anger in her voice. "Neither Mom nor you should have had to go through something like that. You could have been killed!"

"Good thing it didn't happen while my father and uncle were there," Oleg admitted. "Since that episode, I've given it a lot of thought. I think the *garimpo* is coming to an end. Now would be a good time for me to sell my dredge, while we're striking it rich. I think Alemão would buy it if I gave him a good deal. The gold is thinning out, and a lot of dredges take in only 50 or 60 grams every time they process the gold. The way I figure it, though, you need to produce nearly 150 grams to remain economically viable. If you count up dredges and floats, there are more than a thousand rigs operating out there right now."

"If you decide to sell your dredge, I'm not going to stay in the *garimpo* either," Maria put in. "Maybe I can go back to the restaurant at Casa da Lola. My own mission isn't over yet. Alice starts working at the Rondônia State Department of Revenue this month and she'll be able to help out, but Isaías and Lídia will still need me for a while."

The lively talk went on for some time. Towards the end, Alice asked, "Oleg, does your invitation still stand? Is there going to be a Shabbat dinner tomorrow night?"

"Of course. I just need to check and see where exactly. There are only a few Jewish families here, and they usually spend Shabbat together. When I worked at Berimex here in Porto Velho, I got to know the Benesby, Querub, and Bensabá families, and they always invited me. I'm sure I'd still be welcome, and I'd love it if you'd join me."

ΦΦΦ

The following weeks were busy. Oleg went to Palmeiral every Monday morning and came back on the weekend. Once he'd decided to sell the dredge, he offered it to Alemão and some other potential buyers. But selling proved to be more complicated than he'd predicted. After a few weeks of good yield, production fell off sharply and so did Alemão's interest in buying. It was getting harder and harder to prospect. On the one hand, production was low; on the other, the government was erecting ever more barriers. When the waters began nearing their peak in early April and production stopped, as it did every year in that season, Alemão finally showed some interest and offered the same 225 Troy ounces of gold that Oleg had paid Sandra. If Oleg's additional investments were taken into account, the offer really wasn't a good one, but he closed the deal anyway and the dredge was handed over to its new owner. The crew would be the same, except for Maria, who left.

The night that he bid farewell to the *garimpo*, Oleg stayed at Casa da Lola Hotel. As expected, Sandra invited him to take the makeshift elevator up to the second floor.

"This is a special night, Russo. You're going to have the company of four women during this farewell dinner," Sandra said before he'd even gotten off the elevator.

Seated around the large table were Mariana, Maria Bonita, and, to Oleg's surprise, little Camila.

"It's good to see you all, but I didn't expect my friend Camila to be here."

"I thought Maria had told you. Here Camila is at her mother's house and her grandmother's too. She's my granddaughter, Mariana's daughter." Oleg certainly hadn't seen this coming.

"I didn't say anything because I thought you should," replied Maria. "Besides, I haven't had much chance to talk to Russo." She went on, teasing, "I know he's been very concerned about Alice's religious education, but I think he's slow to catch on that she's got a crush on him. Men are either in a big hurry or they drag their heels. Twenty-five years ago, Adriano took so long to see me that I couldn't take it anymore. I was like a panther in a cage!"

"A panther in heat," Sandra countered. "Our friend Amorim says there's just a few things that can't be held back no how, no way: flames going up, water flowing down, and a woman when she wants it."

Everybody laughed. Oleg was struck by the easy way Maria talked about her life. She'd always been very reserved in the *garimpo* and was known to keep a wall between herself and others. Now he realized it was her way of protecting herself from the men who were always pestering her.

"Now that I've sold the dredge and I'm saying my goodbyes to Palmeiral, I can think about my personal life again. Really, Sandra, I had no idea Camila was your granddaughter. Now I know where she gets her blue eyes."

"Russo, don't change the subject. We're talking about Alice. Do you like her?" Sandra was insistent.

"I like her a lot. I'm going to do my best to help her learn about her parents' religion. But for now, that's all. I still don't know what I'm going to do from here on in, and I don't want to get ahead of myself."

"From what I can tell, our Greek god is shy, indecisive, and a tad blind. Well, perhaps as Shabbats go by, things will develop. Maria and Lídia are rooting for you, and together we're going to see that you two tie the knot." Sandra was enjoying herself.

Then she suddenly changed directions. "I'm afraid that in a few years, we'll all have to leave here. The government wants to close down the *garimpos*, which create all sorts of problems. There's a high environmental cost, and crime is getting way out of control. The day there's no more work for Mocha Louca and Niara Nutbuster, I'm going to close Casa da Lola, the one here and the one in Teotônio. My house in Porto Velho is going to be small for so many folks, but we'll figure something out. Maybe I can open up a restaurant in town. With Maria Bonita as head chef, we'd be a hit. Or maybe I'll just retire." Surprising news for everyone.

So that was the story. The big house belonged to Sandra, not Maria. And Alice and Lídia were raising little Camila. It all made sense. The ties between Sandra and Maria ran much deeper than Oleg had imagined. They were ties of friendship but also of cooperation and trust. The peculiar world of the *garimpo* had room for all brands of relationships: beautiful, like this one, or part of that other reality, a harsh and ugly one where there was no room for ethics, morals, or compassion.

What Maria Bonita had said about Alice had come out of left field as far as Oleg was concerned. So far, his relationship with Alice had been one of friendship and a bit of curiosity, with each one wanting to get to know the other one better. Shortly after they'd been introduced, Alice had put up some kind of wall between them and intimated that there was someone else. He hadn't pried. Besides, she was much younger than he was—barely 23. And Oleg had been involved with someone for years. Nothing very serious—more a matter of convenience. He had a kind of relationship with an attractive divorcée named Ana Lúcia, who was in her thirties and had two children to raise. They'd met some years earlier, when Oleg was still manager at Berimex in Rondônia. Ever since, during his rare weekends in Porto Velho, their affection for each other and mutual physical attraction had always carried them off to a round bed in the town's best love motel. They didn't expect much from each other. Just a bit of understanding, some good conversation, and a few hours of relaxation, enough to relieve them of their tensions and do them each a little good. After that first dinner at Maria's house, Oleg hadn't gotten in touch with Ana Lúcia again. He'd preferred to spend Shabbat dinners with Alice. Was he attracted to the girl with those big eyes of some undefined color and those dimples that shone with each smile? Was it possible that he felt something beyond empathy and friendship? Maria Bonita had implied that Alice was interested in him, but he wasn't so sure. He had to keep his head on straight. After all, he was 40 and starting a new life.

"Can you give me and Camila a lift tomorrow?" Maria Bonita asked.

"Sure," he replied. "I'll just say goodbye to Amorim and then we can take off."

The following weekend, there was no Shabbat dinner in the small Porto Velho community. The daughter of one of the state Secretaries was getting married and many in the community had been invited to the wedding; others were traveling and some had gone fishing. That Friday, Oleg arrived at Maria Bonita's earlier than usual and ran into Maria, Lídia, and Camila as they were leaving. They told him that there was a good movie playing and they were in a hurry to get to the cinema, but that Alice had preferred to wait for him for dinner. The scent of intrigue hung so heavy in the air that he was sure the three women were up to something. When he went inside, he found a table set for two, candles lit, two small loaves of challah, and a bottle of wine.

So began Oleg and Alice's first Shabbat and first time alone together.

They were tense at first and the conversation kept falling flat.

"I don't know why," Oleg thought to himself, "but all of a sudden I feel like a teenager out on a date for the first time. I can't think of a thing to say."

Then Alice spilled the beans. "This dinner is a conspiracy by my mother and sister, who cooked the meal and then came up with this story of going out. I want you to know that I'm just as much a victim as you." But she couldn't hide a coy smile.

The ice was broken and the conversation began to flow. Alice asked Oleg about his plans for the future. Choosing his words carefully, Oleg said that at least for the time being, he just wanted to start his new life. He'd just ended a three-year relationship and still didn't know if he was going to stay in Rondônia or go to Manaus, or maybe spend a little time in Israel with his father and brother.

Alice wanted to know more. For one thing, what would his decisions depend on? He didn't answer for a while, as if he were struggling to find the right words. Then he decided to simply skirt the question and ask about her plans.

Alice made a point of telling him that she had a temporary job with the newly created State of Rondônia, where a good dose of skill and willingness to work were welcome. They were quiet for a bit and then she said softly, almost whispering, "I also just left a relationship that didn't have a future."

Then Oleg summoned up his courage and asked with a blush on his face, "Would I have a chance with you, Alice?"

Before saying a word, she smiled and there were those dimples again.

"If you didn't, I wouldn't be here. I just don't know if you can stand to be so close to a panther."

When Maria, Lídia, and Camila got back from the cinema, nobody was home. All they found was a note on the table. "I'm going after happiness," Alice had written.

Maria smiled. "The movie was terrible—but was it worth it!"

ΦΦΦ

When they got to the hotel, Alice was nervous. At the entrance, she bashfully hid behind Oleg, as if all eyes were on her. They hurried up to their room, and she only relaxed after he'd locked the door. But between the four walls, her shyness evaporated, a smile spread over her face again, and without shame or regrets, they gave themselves to each other naturally. In the heat of their pent-up desire, there was neither time nor need for prolonged foreplay. Impatient, they sought to please each other and find the same pleasure for themselves, to use and be used. And this made the night sublime.

Lying in the dark, Oleg couldn't fall asleep. A car would drive by every once in a while, and a little light would break through the window. Alice was sleeping peacefully and it was only then, in the fleeting beam of passing headlights, that he could take in her bare body—before, they'd been perpetually glued to each other. Their lovemaking had been so intense it had left them exhausted. When one had thought they hadn't an ounce of strength left, the other had lent a bit of his or her own, in a delicious game neither wanted to ever end—until Alice had fallen asleep in Oleg's arms, her body entwined around his, where she wanted to stay forever.

Another car drove by, its headlights once again invading the room and affording a vision of Alice's body from a new angle. She had shifted position and Oleg could see her small firm breasts.

"They fit my hands well," he thought. Alice wasn't tall but she was lithe and well-proportioned, her waist so thin it looked like it might break. He was overcome by a feeling of tenderness for this fragile girl. A sensation of tranquility swept over him, and with this peace came sleep.

But just before he dozed off, the thought flit through his head that her eyes—sometimes with hints of gray and blue, other times of green and yellow—looked very much like cat eyes. Or were they the eyes of a panther?

CHAPTER 8
DESTINIES

The economy of Rondônia and even more so of the city of Porto Velho felt the reflections of the slow death of the *garimpos* on the Madeira River. Sad reminders of days of plenty, dredges were abandoned one after the other, leaving cemeteries of scrap metal along the riverbanks. For a while, the local economy was totally dependent on public service jobs and public works projects.

Two years had passed since Sandra Reis closed her once glorious Casa da Lola floating brothels in Palmeiral and Teotônio and moved to Porto Velho. She had gone to live in her spacious home in the city, together with her daughter Mariana and granddaughter Camila, now 16. Amorim had closed up his shop and left the *garimpo* around the same time. He and Renato went to live on the family ranch on highway BR-364, not far from town. In addition to raising cattle and planting cacao, they had another promising business: fish farming. It was a growing activity and looked to be a good economic alternative for the region. Amorim's sons had recognized that this new business held tremendous potential and they'd transformed the ranch's natural lakes into gigantic fish tanks.

Despite Brazil's inflation and economic instability, agribusiness was flourishing on the fertile lands of Rondônia and opening up new prospects for a much hardier economy. Although many people had made money during the heyday of the *garimpos*, their success had been short-lived. In their stubborn insistence on sticking with it, countless successful prospectors lost all they had. Sandra and Amorim were among the few who had prospered during the golden days of the *garimpos* and managed to protect part of their earnings. Curiously, neither had worked directly with gold prospecting itself but had provided services to the prospectors.

Unlike Sandra, who was healthy—paraplegia aside—Amorim wasn't in good shape. He suffered from asthma, gastritis, sinus trouble, and rheumatism and, like everybody else in the *garimpo*, malaria had attacked him at least half a dozen times. Still, his son Renato religiously drove him over to his friend Sandra's once a week for their traditional card game. While Renato waited for his father in Porto Velho, he'd use the time to go out with Mariana—for some ice-cream, or to take in a movie, or whatever. That was the justification accepted by all, but with a good dose of teasing. It was a longstanding relationship that everyone knew about yet had never been made official. Rumor always had it that Camila was actually Renato's daughter. Sixteen years earlier, when Camila had been born out of wedlock to an unknown father, Renato was married and had two children. His marriage wasn't going well, and one day his wife just up and left both husband and children. Ever since, Renato and Mariana had been involved in this peculiar relationship, where he lived with his children and she, with her mother. The multitude of films they'd supposedly seen together and the gallons of ice-cream enjoyed over the course of those many years fed a lot of good-natured joking. On some occasions, the couple would get back from the cinema, or maybe from the ice-cream shop, so late—in the wee hours of the morning—that Amorim had to sleep on the couch in Sandra's living room.

During one of their weekly card games, Sandra came up with an idea that her friend approved on the spot. It was late October 1993, not long before Amorim's 70th birthday—an excellent reason to invite their friends for a barbecue at his family's ranch. After Oleg had left the *garimpo*, he'd spent some months in Israel and then he and Alice had moved to Manaus, where they opened up a small river cargo business. Busy with their new work, plus a young son to look after and another baby on the way, it had been a while since they'd visited Rondônia. In recent years, Licco had been practically incommunicado; he spent most of his days taking care of his rosewood plantation in Maués, where he didn't have a phone. Amorim had tried to reach him several times at the Berimex office in Manaus but he'd always been told the same thing: "Leave your name and number and Licco will get back to you." Licco did return his calls, but as time went by, they'd had less and less contact.

It took Amorim a few days to determine the precise whereabouts of the folks he wanted to invite and get in touch with them. Roberto confirmed right away, since he'd been planning to visit his father for his 70th birthday anyway. What's more, for him the party would be a good excuse for meeting up with Maria Bonita again. One year after the Prainha War, she'd accepted his invitation to visit him in Scotland. Since then, the *cabocla* from Purus River and the professor of medieval history had seen each other quite often.

Other guests likewise confirmed their presence right away. Some, like Alice and Oleg, couldn't make it. Oleg's father had died suddenly of a massive stroke in September, just the month before, and the couple had traveled to join the rest of the family in Israel. His brother David's death had shaken Licco deeply, and he had decided to stay on in Maués for a while rather than accompanying the others to Israel. In fact, his brother's premature death had upset Licco so much that he seemed to remain in a state of shock for several days. He simply couldn't accept the fact that David had passed away right when everything suggested he'd finally reached a phase of joy and happiness after a life of much turmoil.

Much to David's immense satisfaction, Oleg had put an end to his adventure in the *garimpo* and married Alice. His first grandson, Elia, had come along soon after and it would not be long before a second joined him. David's younger son, Dov, had served in the Israeli

Army and just earned his engineering degree. Respected and admired, David was active in the leadership of the kibbutz where he lived with his wife Ester, a successful painter. Licco had been so distressed by these and a few other personal problems that he decided that Amorim's invitation would offer a chance for a little respite; later, when he felt up to it, he'd join his brother's family in Israel. So his presence at Amorim's party was confirmed.

ΦΦΦ

Licco went straight from the Porto Velho airport to Sandra Reis' home. He needed to get some things off his chest and ask his friend for advice. He had hit a rough patch and she might have the answers to his questions.

When young Camila opened the door, Licco was taken aback by the radical change in the woman seated in the wheelchair. Her hair was no longer the color of fire, nor was Sandra wearing the flashy clothes that had been her trademark back in the *garimpo*. She looked like a sweet little old lady, discretely dressed and with well-coiffed gray hair. Her only dash of flamboyance was some light lipstick.

At the age of 70, this was a fitting image for Sandra Reis, the tennis player from fifty years earlier, back in Manaus. The thought went through Licco's mind that nothing about her evoked the scandalous madam of a brothel in the *garimpo*. The only thing that remained unchanged were her blue eyes, which still lit up her face, now covered in wrinkles unconcealed by any makeup.

How could they be expected to contain their emotions? For a few moments, it seemed that Sandra would cry but she pulled herself together and even smiled. "Licco, my friend! I can tell you're surprised by my new look. This way no one recognizes me and I'm not a target of everyone's bias against people who work—or who once worked—in the sex trade. I was so very sorry to hear about your brother. It's a pity Alice and Oleg won't be coming. At least you're here, and Roberto arrives tomorrow. His relationship with Maria Bonita was the best thing to come out of the Prainha War."

Licco was clueless. "What war are you talking about, my dear?"

Sandra was startled. "You never heard about the war? No point keeping it a secret anymore. The years have gone by, everyone escaped safe and sound, and it even produced a happy couple. It's a story worth telling." And so Sandra did, with a good dose of pride in her voice. Oleg had led the massive counter-attack with matchless skill and won the battle, which had come to be known in the prospecting world as the Prainha War. The glory had been his, but without Sandra's help, the outcome could have been markedly different.

"Well, at the end, when it was clear they'd won, Maria Bonita celebrated by shooting off one last round of fireworks—and then grabbed the only man around her and planted a big smack right on his lips. The lucky fellow was Amorim's son, Roberto." Sandra finished off her tale with a laugh. "It seems they both liked it so much that they haven't stopped kissing since!"

"Nobody had the courage to tell me this ghastly story! It's the first time I've heard it. It seems I'm always the last to know," Licco said in exasperation. "That aside, I'm happy for Maria Bonita. If anyone deserves happiness, it's her. Oleg and Alice couldn't come, but I intend to represent them in style. After Amorim's birthday, I'm off to Israel to stay with the family too. And I'm planning a trip to Bulgaria. I've still got a lot of friends over there and I want to see how the country's adopting to democracy, now that communism is dead. It'll take years to repair the country's economic base— everything's rusted and obsolete, not to mention the changes in mentality that'll be needed. On their way back from Israel, Alice and Oleg are coming to Porto Velho to visit you all. They miss you!"

"Maria Bonita told me. Now that she's Oleg's mother-in-law, they've grown real close and she spends most of her time in Manaus. I knew it had to be something real serious for Alice and Oleg to turn down Amorim's invitation. I can only imagine how sad and shaken you all are. I spent just a few days with David but that was enough to grow to like him."

Sandra said nothing for a few moments and then switched tones. "Amazing how the world turns! It's almost certain that Maria and Roberto are going to make a life together, and she'll be Amorim's daughter-in-law. When you met him in the *garimpo*, you never could've imagined that one day you'd be relatives. If my daughter Mariana and Renato ever get over this silly business of 'going to the movies' and 'having ice-cream' and finally make it official, even I'll be part of the family." Sandra chuckled.

"David was more than a brother to me," Licco said. "We were orphaned very young and I helped raise him. I was almost a father to him. During World War II, he managed to escape the labor camp and join the resistance. He was arrested, tortured, and almost died—but he survived. After Germany was defeated, he became an important figure in Bulgaria, as a member of the Communist Party. That's when Oleg was born. Over time, David, once a young idealist, grew disillusioned with the regime he'd helped create. The dream was over, and the harsh reality was that the Communist regime was a dictatorship just as bloody as fascism. Any original or independent thinking, even if it differed only a little from the ideas of the helmsmen of the nations—as they liked to call the Marxist-Leninist leaders—was heresy and a crime that had to be eradicated. David's disenchantment became complete when he was accused of industrial espionage and sentenced to serve years as a traitor. David got out of prison in 1974, when Berta and I organized his and Oleg's escape to the West. It's a long story!"

Sandra was clearly moved. "You'd told me a bit about your brother's life but I didn't know this last part. I was amazed—horrified actually—by the story of the human pendulum. David's life was utterly fascinating."

Licco was quiet for a time, and Sandra felt something else was bothering him. Finally he spoke up.

"As if my brother's early death were not enough, I've got another problem and I need your advice, Sandra. You're not going to believe it." Licco paused before saying, "A woman."

The confession stunned Sandra. She couldn't imagine this man with anyone other than Berta. Her image of that perfect couple was part of her memories of the good old days with Ricardo, and she didn't want anything about that to change.

Saddened, Sandra took a guess. "A much younger woman, is that it?" She could tell from the expression on his face that she'd hit the mark. "That's always been men's weak spot, especially when they get past 50 and reach their midlife crisis. I always thought you were one of the few men vaccinated against this type of event. Well, spit it out, my friend! Go on, I'm all ears."

And Licco told her the story of the young elementary school teacher, Laura, whom he'd known since she was a little girl. He told her about the tragic death of Laura's parents and sister and how he had given her shelter and protection in those hard times. He told her how he'd come down with malaria and how the young Laura had diligently and tenderly taken care of him, fighting to save his life.

"At first, she was like a daughter to me. But then our feelings gradually changed... I don't know how a 20-year-old girl can be physically attracted to a 70-year-old man, but I know the opposite is possible. Your friend Licco is head over heels in love with the woman."

Sandra fidgeted in the wheelchair. "Your problem, my friend, is quite a thorny one. But not as bad as I might have thought. At least, your little teacher friend doesn't appear to want to take advantage of you. We women always seek the security and protection that men can provide us. Just imagine—this needy young girl, an orphan, alone in the world, finds a mature, kind, loving man—a little worn around the edges, that's true, but still in pretty fine shape—and she seeks shelter under his protective wings. Laura has quite likely fallen more for her protector's prodigious brain than his body. So what!? That too is love."

"How long can this love last, Sandra? I don't have the courage to trick or lie to someone I love. Since I'm older and more mature, I can see farther down the road than she can. I try not to look at the glass bottle but at the liquid inside. In a few years, I'll be a decrepit old man and Laura, my nurse. I can't and won't destroy her life. Especially because she dreams of having children." Licco's voice was sad. "I fled Maués—I asked for some time to think, but truth be told, I'm fleeing disaster in the guise of happiness. And that hurts bad."

Sandra didn't reply. She felt oddly weary, and she excused herself, saying she needed to lie down. They agreed to continue the conversation the next day, on their way to Amorim's farm in Sandra's wheelchair-equipped car.

Before Licco left, she asked him, "And my mother's manuscripts? Are they safely stored?"

"They're in my safe at home, and Oleg and Daniel have instructions on how to proceed when I pass away. I read them attentively; some of it was quite surprising. I have one question. Do you know Sara Rosales' real name?"

"I thought it would go unnoticed." Sandra's voice was strained. "Yes, Licco, I do. The original name of Sara Rosales, my real mother, was Esther Blumenfeld—Rifca Blumenfeld's youngest sister. On the trip from Poland to South America, the two sisters were part of the same 'remounting' sent to Manaus. The younger sister entrusted her daughter, for whom she couldn't care, to her older sister, Tamara Melo. I'm my aunt's daughter—or, to put it another way, I'm my own cousin. And now, Licco, I have no more secrets."

As fate would have it, neither the trip to Amorim's farm nor his party was to be. Just like her mother years earlier, Sandra Reis went to bed and didn't wake up the next morning. Mariana found her in the same position as always. She looked peaceful, but her body was cold despite the Amazonian heat.

ΦΦΦ

"Mariana's in the other room. Renato is helping with the funeral arrangements. I'd love to get together with you under happier circumstances, my dear friend," said Amorim, and Licco could tell the little man was very upset—pushed to his limits in fact. Licco had stopped by Sandra's to say goodbye to Mariana; from there he was heading directly to the airport. The last days hadn't been easy and he was weary and tired.

"These are bleak times I'm going through," Licco thought. "I want to console my friend, but I have absolutely nothing to say. In such a short span of time, I've lost my brother and now Sandra. And on top of it, at my age, I'm living an impossible love story, a love without any future at all. And I barely had a chance to get any advice from Sandra."

More people came in and the two men stood there in silence a while longer. Then the door opened again and Licco saw Maria Bonita enter, a little older but as pretty as ever. When she spotted him, she rushed over to give him a hug. It was an affectionate gesture, like a girl embracing her father after a long absence. Maria's green eyes were still lovely and even though sad they seemed to smile.

"This professor of medieval history is awfully lucky," Licco thought. He felt tears coming to his eyes and tried to cover them up, chiding himself for turning into an old softie.

"Now you've got time for nothing but Maués," she replied. "I spent six months in Manaus, met your whole family, but you never showed up."

Licco thought he heard a touch of mischief in Maria Bonita's voice. "I suppose," he pondered to himself, "everybody already knows about my affair with Laura, and my friends must be enjoying a big laugh about the size of the horns she'll put on my head in a few years."

Maria hugged Amorim just as affectionately, and Licco had the impression he choked back a sob. Then Mariana came in carrying a small envelope. Her eyes were red from crying, but to Licco she seemed amazingly serene and strong. She quickly turned to Amorim. "Vicente, my mother had come up with a little joke for your birthday. She was writing a letter, but unfortunately she didn't get to put the finishing touches on it. She cared a lot about you and I really want you to accept this last gift she left." Mariana opened the envelope and took out a letter that had been typed on stationery bearing the letterhead of the City of Porto Velho. She began reading aloud:

> *Dear Mr. Vicente Amorim,*
> *Be it hereby declared that you are summoned to appear at the Porto Velho municipal crematorium, located at 7855 Calama Avenue, oven no. 165, armed with ten gallons of gasoline or one cord of firewood, on the eighth day of November of the present year, at the time of*

7:00 am, for the purpose of cremation pursuant to a unanimous decision handed down by the Citizenship Committee of the Municipal Chambers of this fair city.

Upon receipt of this letter, you are unconditionally banned from imbibing any alcoholic beverage or any type of medication so as to avoid uncontrolled combustion or explosion.

Tardiness of more than thirty minutes will result in an initial fine of one hundred dollars, with an additional fifty dollars imposed for each further one-hour delay.

Due to your advanced age and low weight (which accounts for your nickname, Pounder), and given that you can now be considered an absolute public 'inutility', you are hereby exempted from paying the municipal tax applicable to this procedure.

Amorim's face lit up in a contagious grin and soon everyone was laughing. Mariana went on. "I found the letter in my mother's typewriter. Now I understand why she'd been bugging so many people just to get a few pieces of stationery from City Hall. A strange twist of fate: her funeral will be tomorrow, November 8, the same date she'd scheduled for your cremation, Vicente."

186

CHAPTER 9
I, MARIA

Twenty-three years ago, walking alongside a cart filled with rubber *pelas*, I left Quatro Ases behind. Tata and Isaías—he was six then—padded alongside me, while Alice and Lídia took turns on top of the *pelas*. I went back once, in the company of a rubber tapper who had worked with Adriano and Benjamin; we picked up the rest of the *pelas*. I sold them off one by one and used the money to build a small house on the edge of Fortaleza do Abunã. I used the rest to lease a spot overlooking the Abunã River, where I sold snacks and pastries that we made at home.

Somehow we managed to survive. We were poor but not destitute, and we never went hungry. I was never one for just twiddling my thumbs. I was willing to take on any kind of work and I even did some odd jobs for the mayor's wife. Over the years, I had some suitors, but Adriano was always very much present in my mind and I didn't want to even think about another man. I preferred to take care of my children and accompany them in their studies, while I learned more myself. I had never been to school when I was a child. I only learned to read when I was 16, with Adriano's help. My textbooks were yesterday's newspapers—and some were even older than that, ones that had been used as wrapping. Later on, in the rubber groves, Dona Nina taught me some basic math.

Our first year in Fortaleza de Abunã was really tough on me and the kids. After a few weeks, Alice finally understood that her parents and brother hadn't just gone away for a little while—they were never coming back. The girl couldn't wrap her mind around the whole tragedy. Her muffled little sobs cut me to the quick; they left me sad and upset. In a way, her pain made ours easier. I was so busy with the tasks of everyday life and so worried about the kids that I didn't have time for my own suffering. Night after night, Alice would fall asleep in the only place she was able to—my arms; when she finally did nod off, the nightmares would come. Isaías and Lídia seemed to understand that under the circumstances, Alice was our priority. We all loved the little girl hard, until time softened her wounds.

And so we got on with our lives, each helping as best as possible and all of us looking to each other for support. I've always been the proud mother of three children, and I love them all equally. We were traumatized by the tragic things that happened in the rubber groves; they marked us for the rest of our lives. Fortunately, we didn't have much time to feel sorry for ourselves. We were forced to stifle our pain, dry up out tears, and march on. Me, the uneducated *cabocla* from the Purus River, kept things together. I worked hard, the kids accompanied me, and we all learned a valuable lesson together: even in the midst of bad times, we have to face our problems head-on and do more and better than expected. Today I'd venture to say we all came out winners.

The public school in Fortaleza de Abunã was very poor, but it did have a teacher and some books. Thanks to her, my kids learned to read and write early on, including some math. We sat by lamplight every evening, doing homework. Those nights, I became a hard-working student myself. We led a simple life, and quite a poor one, but the kids grew up healthy and even though they didn't have a father, they had the advantage of a tight-knit family.

I remember one event so well: Isaías was 14 when the mayor's wife summoned me and asked me to fix a lunch for twenty people, members of the entourage that came along with the new governor of the Territory of Rondônia, Colonel Jorge Teixeira. I'm a good cook; I was just a girl when I started working at Dona Neide's restaurant in Surara, on the Purus River. So that day I cooked up an assortment of regional dishes using a bunch of different fish, and the luncheon was a hit. Dona Aída, the governor's wife, was delighted. She came into the kitchen to congratulate me and thank me for the great food. I guess she liked me, because before the entourage left town, she came back and asked if I'd be interested in moving to Porto Velho, where I'd work as a cook at the governor's mansion, as an employee of the state. I'd have a real contract and full benefits. She said she'd help me buy a house and enroll the kids in school. I didn't think twice, and I didn't ask any questions! In January 1980, I hurried to sell our little house, and off we went to Porto Velho, a little scared and apprehensive but full of hope. The hardest thing about the sudden move was that we had to say goodbye to our brave dog Tata. She'd just given birth to a litter and we couldn't take her along. She stayed with our neighbor, who really liked her, and that made it easier to bid farewell to a companion of so many years.

During those years, Dona Aída and Colonel Teixeira were very important in my life. Without their help, we wouldn't have been able to buy our house and the kids wouldn't have studied in the best schools in Porto Velho. The colonel had been the head of the Military School in Manaus and he really knew how important a good school is in a young person's life. When Isaías graduated from high school with honors, the colonel didn't hesitate—he helped move him to São Paulo (flew him down in a Brazilian Air Force plane) and arranged lodging for him at a friend's house. And so Isaías took the entrance exam for medicine and was accepted by one of the top public universities in Brazil. During Isaías' early years in college, the colonel and Dona Aída helped him on various other occasions. In 1986, when Isaías was in his second year of medical school, the governor's term of office was up and so our paths went off in different directions. Colonel Teixeirão went to live in Rio de Janeiro and even teased me about how much he'd miss my cooking. I never saw him again.

The new governor had his own cook, and since I didn't have job stability, I was out of work. I needed to find another source of income and fast. It wasn't easy to support a son studying in São Paulo and a home with two younger students in Porto Velho. With the help of the girls, I went back to baking pastries, and so we went on with our lives. Until one day, when Dona Sandra sent her messenger to me. Dona Sandra owned the finest nightclub in the city and needed a cook for her establishment, which was right downtown. It was the best job offer I'd had. The first time I met Dona Sandra, sitting in that wheelchair of hers, I confess I was a little scared, especially because there was a rumor that she'd had her ex-husband killed. Even so I took the job; I didn't really have any other choice. Over time, I got to know Dona Sandra and gradually discovered the sweet person hidden behind the mask of a tough whorehouse madam.

Some months later, she opened the Casa da Lola floating hotel and restaurant in the Teotônio *garimpo* and invited me to work there. The salary was much better: 15 grams of gold a month. I'd never make so much in town. I accepted on the spot—I needed the money for my kids. One time in the *garimpo*, Dona Sandra heard a man offer me the exact same 15 grams for a night of sex. It was common for cooks to supplement their earnings like that, for much less even. When the fellow left, Sandra asked why I'd turned down that small fortune, and then I told her a bit about my life, up until Adriano's death and our departure from Quatro Ases. From that day on, Dona Sandra treated me differently. She insisted on visiting my home in the city, the one I'd bought and paid for with the help of Colonel Teixeirão, and so she ended up meeting my daughters, Alice and Lídia. Then she made a surprising offer: my girls would move into her big, roomy house in Porto Velho—on the sole condition that we take care of her granddaughter, Camila. The girl needed to study and Mariana didn't have anyone to leave her with in town. It was obvious that Dona Sandra liked my girls. And it was a good arrangement for us. Alice and Lídia would live in a nicer house, in a better neighborhood and closer to their schools. And I could rent out my house and use the money towards Isaías' college costs in São Paulo. It all worked so well that we were soon friends and confidants. Dona Sandra always helped me out, and I did the same whenever I could.

Then Oleg came along, a good-looking, ambitious, well-mannered young man. When Dona Sandra discovered he was the nephew of her long-ago friend Licco, she got more excited than I'd ever seen her and she decided to help the young fellow, who she called a Greek god. He wanted to go into prospecting and was looking to buy a dredge. Coincidentally, Dona Sandra had a suction dredge at the Palmeiral *garimpo* that had been out of operation for months, just waiting for a buyer. She sold it cheap to Oleg and then asked me to go work

there. She wanted to know about everything that happened on the dredge. It was almost like Oleg was her
son. He paid really good. In a few months, I was earn-
ing 30 grams of gold cooking and washing the crew's
clothes, so all of a sudden I had more than enough money—something I'd never had before. I worked with him
a year and I can say in all confidence that he is a good,
honest, decent, and very smart fellow. Today Oleg is
married to my daughter Alice, and I'm very proud of
my son-in-law.

While I was still living in the *garimpo*, I took part in
the famous Prainha War. Fortunately, none of us were
hurt, but five men on the other side were killed and another five went to jail. We were really lucky because
Sandra warned us we were going to be attacked. We
managed to duly prepare ourselves and surprise the
gunmen, who didn't expect the "warm welcome" we
gave them. Roberto and I spent the night atop the
riverbank, providing cover. We set off the fireworks
that left our attackers visible in the light. Ever since my
childhood on Lake Igapó-Mirim, my senses have been
sharp, probably because of my indigenous ancestry. I
don't know how to explain it, but I really can see things
most people can't and I instinctively feel the presence
of strangers. And so, in the middle of the dark night,
from atop the riverbank, before anyone else, I spotted—
better, I felt—the gunmen approaching in their boats. I
fired the warning shot while Roberto set off the fireworks. With all those colorful lights, the battle looked

more like a party—except that people died at the party. Life isn't worth much in the *garimpo*. Every once in a while, a corpse would wash down the river, carried by the current. It was almost a routine event. We were rather indifferent about it, at most asking ourselves what the lifeless body had done to deserve such a sad end.

Following those adventure-filled years of prosperity came the bust, when hundreds of dredges were abandoned and the riverbanks became gloomy cemeteries for what was left, huge mountains of scrap metal. Oleg and I were lucky to get out of the *garimpo* at the right time.

My later-in-life relationship with Roberto helped me mature and become more self-confident and patient. I can hardly believe that after twenty years with no men in my life, I'm dating again. I'd forgotten that love can be so tender and nice. It all started the night Casa da Lola was inaugurated, in the Palmeiral *garimpo*. After dinner, I hitched a ride in Amorim's boat. It was quite late and I had to start work early the next day. I sat down next to Roberto and we headed back. Halfway there, I felt his hand rest on mine. I tried to shift position but he wouldn't move his hand and I realized his touch wasn't accidental. He avoided looking at me. He was embarrassed and practically had his back to me, but he didn't let go of my hand. And I felt the affection in his touch. We couldn't figure out what to do; we just sat there like that for a good while. I was surprised by how much pleasure this physical contact gave me. In the *garimpo*, this sort of thing is unusual. People think about sex, not about real feelings and affection. Our relationship was born from the glances we had stolen at each other over that dinner and from that casual touch. By the time of the Prainha War, we'd been dating for some weeks.

Oleg teases me by saying that if Roberto really wants to win me over, he'll have to change jobs. History, OK, but medieval history—no way in Brazil! It's a joke, but bottom line, there's some truth to it. Although I love Scotland in the summer, I can't stand Europe's cold winters. Roberto knows this and he wants me to be happy, so he's looking for some way to come back to Brazil, maybe teach at a university here. Meanwhile, I spend summers in Scotland and he comes to Rondônia for Christmas and New Year's.

Some things changed after Dona Sandra passed away. Mariana and Renato finally quit pretending and formally admitted that he's Camila's father. They're married now and don't need to go to the movies or out for ice-cream every night.

Other things changed for the worse. Vicente Amorim never got over the loss of his dear friend and card partner. He's in poor health and in such low spirits that he hardly tells jokes anymore—his former trademark.

I worry about Licco too. I guess the years are starting to weigh on him, and he doesn't go to Maués to take care of his rosewood plantation so often. Now he spends most of his time reading and listening to music at his home in Manaus. Not long ago, Oleg mentioned that a few years after Berta passed away, his uncle had fallen in love with a much younger woman. The disappointment he suffered in that relationship was apparently what had left him so downcast. I think it's an off-limits subject for the Hazan family, and I've never asked about it again. Whenever I go to spend a few days with Alice and Oleg in Manaus, I visit Licco and we talk for hours. For some reason I can't quite explain, he makes me feel safe, at ease, and at peace, and I know he enjoys having me around. I worry because even though he's in good health and the family really watches out for him, I've found him even lonelier and sadder than usual.

My children are all grown up now. Dr. Isaías lives in São Paulo, where he works at a well-known hospital and doesn't have time for anything, not even girls. He wanted to come along on our upcoming trip to Fortaleza de Abunã and Quatro Ases, but the life of a young doctor, especially at the start of his career, is rough. Even though Lídia doesn't recall much about our lives in the rubber groves, she really wants to visit her father's grave. I've told so many stories about the beauty of the river, its waterfalls and beaches, the virgin forests, the singing of the birds and calls of the monkeys—well, her expectations are big. She's a nationally known journalist. She lives with Isaías in São Paulo and, just like him, thinks about nothing but her career. I'm so proud of my kids' success. For a simple cook who never went to school and was widowed very early on, I think I did all right. I've only got one grandson so far, but the second is on his way. Big belly and all, Alice has also insisted on coming back to Quatro Ases with us. She's never said anything but I know her well and I know she wants to bid a final farewell to Nina, Benjamin, and Ariel.

ΦΦΦ

Last year, I made another dream of mine come true: Over a long holiday weekend, I got Oleg and Alice to go back to Purus River with me, where I was born and grew up. It took nearly twelve hours by boat from Manaus to Lake Surara, a place that was once so important to me. The trip really got to me, especially because the lake is as lovely as ever and the landscape practically untouched. The houseboat where I lived with Adriano isn't there anymore, but the vegetation and beach are just the same. My eyes filled with tears, memories washed over me, and a sweet remembrance floated up from the recesses of my mind: the enchanted place where I, still just a young girl, seduced Adriano— almost at force—and happily lost my virginity. When I remember the scene, I can't help but smile.

We went to Lake Igapó-Mirim too, and I discovered that Surara wasn't nearly as far away as I'd thought. Over twenty years earlier, it had taken Adriano and me several days to cover the same distance, paddling along with the help of the Purus River current. Now, equipped with an outboard motor, we got there in a few hours, even though the current was against us this time. When we entered the long channel that leads from the river to the lake, scenes of my childhood flashed before my eyes like in a movie. Time had really stopped there. Nothing had changed. We saw trees hundreds of years old along the way. The fact that I recognized them really got to me. And to my surprise, gray river dolphins surfaced in the same spot where I'd watched them playing years before. When I heard the cry of the toucan calling his mate, I looked around for him, and just like every single day when I was a kid, I saw the colorful bird hidden in the green branches. Everything was just like I remembered it. I felt as if I'd left that enchanted place only a few days before. The big difference is that nobody lives on the lake anymore. We went to the spot where my house used to be and to the place where I got into Adriano's canoe, but we didn't find anything. Not a single log of old possumwood or any other sign that people had once lived there. It was clear that the former inhabitants had left the lake years earlier. We asked about my mother on nearby lakes, in Paricatuba, and even farther away, in Apuí, but no one remembered Dona Eulália. The people we talked to asked for the last name of the person we were looking for, but I didn't know. This seems unbelievable today, but it's the absolute truth—I never knew my mother's or my stepfather's last names. I stared hard at every single *caboclo* who crossed our path, because I probably had a brother or sister among them, who I'd never even recognize.

ΦΦΦ

So many years later, we're finally headed back to Quatro Ases *seringal* to complete my journey into the past. Here we are in Fortaleza do Abunã—it's changed so much! The waterfall is the same, but a good deal of the town has electricity now, streets have been laid, and interstate highway BR-364 has been paved. It's so easy to get to Porto Velho or Rio Branco now. So much easier to reach the rubber forests. Way back when, you had to make two overnight stops to get here from Quatro Ases. We've located our old neighbors and even met Tata's granddaughter—white with big black spots, just like her ancestor. As if in a dream, I keep returning to an image that is etched in my memory: the little girls Lídia and Alice running down the street after the mutt. And as if they are watching the same movie, the two of them—grown women now—start playing the same game. The dog joins in, wagging her tail in happiness, running in circles for a bit and then letting herself get caught. As eager for affection as her grandmother, she revels in being petted and scratched behind the ears. I give our neighbor a hug and break into tears. Before we leave, Alice orders a female puppy when the dog has its next litter. I don't even need to ask; I already know what the family's future darling will be called. Lídia and Alice enjoy every last moment of this return to the childhood that they'll hold onto forever in their memories.

Our former neighbors were quick to warn us not to expect much from our return to Quatro Ases because the rubber forests no longer exist as we once knew them. Almost all of them have new owners, and everything revolves around agriculture and livestock raising now.

Our pickup follows a road that isn't paved but at least it's graveled, and we make good time. I don't recognize a thing around me, but I can tell we're getting closer and my heart starts beating faster. As we round the last bend, I see a huge pasture and right smack in the middle, amazingly, I spot the old ceiba tree that shaded Benjamin Melul's house. Cattle graze around the majestic tree, seeking relief from the heat. No signs remain, but I know that somewhere nearby, a little off to the right of the giant ceiba, Adriano, Benjamin, Nina, and Ariel lie buried. May they rest in peace!

Try as I might, I can't figure out where the house that once was our home and where Isaías and Lídia were born would have stood. I can't believe my eyes. There's nothing, absolutely nothing, left of the forest that reigned supreme here twenty years ago. I'm so disappointed I'm speechless. I turn around to look at Alice and Lídia and see the same expression of total disappointment on their faces. It's just as well Isaías didn't come along. We walk in silence towards the river and I realize that the signs of erosion left by the missing forest are unmistakable. Once again, man's presence is bringing destruction.

When I reach the river's edge, atop the high bank, I spot a tiny white-sand beach. The river curves sharply to the left, and on the other side, a little higher upstream, a smaller river flows into the Abunã, coming from the highlands of Bolivia. My heart starts racing. Now I can visualize it. It was there, in that exact spot, twenty-three years ago, that a massive wall of floodwaters ripped up age-old trees and destroyed everything in its path, carrying off the boat with our precious balls of rubber and changing our lives forever.

GLOSSARY

banho: a weekend property on the edge of the city, crisscrossed by the crystal-clear waters of idyllic streams, where its owners seek refuge from the muggy days of an equatorial summer

brabo: someone new to the *garimpo*, who doesn't know anything about extracting gold; a greenhorn

caboclo (*cabocla*: f., sing.; *caboclos*: m., pl.; caboclas: f., pl.): 1. an individual of mixed European and indigenous ethnicity; 2. a native of the Amazon region

cachaça: a rum-type liquor made from sugar cane

cruzeiro: the Brazilian currency at the time the novel takes place

despesca: the process of separating out gold by washing the material brought up from the riverbed, transferring it to a centrifuge, and then adding and burning off mercury so that only gold remains

fofoca: agglomeration of barges and dredges at a prospecting site; prospecting site itself *garimpo*: gold-mining operations or any prospecting region in the Amazon (*garimpeiro*: prospector)

Ladino: language spoken by the Jews who were expelled from the Iberian Peninsula by the Inquisition in the late fifteenth century; also called Judeo-Spanish

manso: experienced prospector

pela: ball of rubber, weighing roughly 100 pounds

stille chuppah: a Yiddish term that literally means "silent, or quiet, wedding"; it refers to an unregistered ceremony without the presence of a rabbi

suction dredge: a dredge that removes material from a riverbed by digging into the bed and sucking material up through a hose; some can reach down to a depth of 100 feet

voadeira: motorboat used to tug a dredge or as a means of transportation

Zwi Migdal: an organized crime group that trafficked women, mostly Jews from Eastern Europe, to South America in the late nineteenth and early twentieth centuries

ABOUT THE AUTHOR

ILKO MINEV was born and grew up in Sofia, Bulgaria, where he received his degree in German studies. He also studied economics in Belgium before immigrating to Brazil. After spending time in Sao Paulo, he moved to Manaus, where he quite literally fell in love and put down roots. There he made a career as a business executive and served as Honorary Consul for the Netherlands for more than thirty years. He is married and has two children and two grandchildren.